WHAT HIS MONEY CAN'T HIDE

BY
MAGGIE COX

MILLS &
BOON®

First published in Great Britain 2012
by Mills & Boon, an imprint of Harlequin (UK) Limited.
Harlequin (UK) Limited, Eton House, 18-24 Paradise Road,
Richmond, Surrey TW9 1SR

© Maggie Cox 2012

ISBN: 978 0 263 89137 9

Harlequin (UK) policy is to use papers that are natural, renewable
and recyclable products and made from wood grown in sustainable
forests. The logging and manufacturing process conform to the
legal environmental regulations of the country of origin.

Printed and bound in Spain
by Blackprint CPI, Barcelona

WHAT HIS MONEY CAN'T HIDE

CHAPTER ONE

'Is THE old place just how you remember it, Mr Ashton?'

The innocently asked question from his chauffeur Jimmy, as he drove Drake to his less than agreeable destination cut him open like a knife. *Yes...his home town was just as dreary and dismal as he remembered it. His memory hadn't lied.*

Glancing out through the tinted car windows, noting the rundown buildings and general sense of despair that hung like a gloomy pall in the air, he felt a sensation in the pit of his stomach right then that was very close to nauseous. Was he insane even to *think* of revisiting this place, when it had caused him nothing but heartache and pain? It beggared belief that he had agreed his firm of architects would accept a commission from the government to create affordable, aesthetically pleasing housing to attract new residents to the area.

Drake put it down to a moment of insanity. Why anyone in their right mind would want to live in such a soulless *pit* he couldn't begin to fathom. As his grey eyes stared hard at the drab scenes that flew by the backs of his eyes burned with remembered pain.

Snapping out of his reverie, he realised that Jimmy

was still waiting for an answer. 'Yes, I'm sorry to say it's *exactly* how I remember it.'

'Certainly looks like it could use a facelift.' The broad good-natured face reflected in the driving mirror displayed his sympathy.

'Where did you grow up, Jimmy?' Drake asked him.

'I was born and bred in Essex. The family didn't have a lot of money but we pulled together. Had plenty of laughs along the way, as well as tears.' He grinned.

Drake forced a smile. He wished he could have said the same about his own upbringing, but sadly there had been very few laughs in his home after his mother had walked out. His father had raised him, but he'd done it with an angry and bitter resentment that had made Drake wary of making too many demands. Even the most basic requests had been apt to enrage his father and make him particularly cruel. Very quickly he'd learned to be self-sufficient and resourceful…simply because he'd *had* to.

Enough of this pointless and painful introspection!

Scowling, he leant towards the driver's seat. 'Pull over at the end of the high street, then go and park, Jimmy. I've just spied a coffee place and I'm in need of some caffeine and food. I've also got to look over some papers. Give me at least a couple of hours and I'll ring you to come and pick me up.'

'Sure thing, Mr Ashton. Do you want to take your newspaper with you?'

'Thanks.'

The aroma of rich roast coffee acted like a siren, reeling Drake in as he pushed open the heavy glass door of the café he'd noticed and entered. Years ago, when he was a schoolboy, this old Victorian building had housed the newsagents where his dad had bought his newspaper and tobacco, and later—when it had become a mini-supermarket—his cans of beer too...

The bittersweet memory was apt to sour Drake's anticipated enjoyment of his breakfast, so he jettisoned it to the back of his mind in the same way he ruthlessly eliminated unwanted e-mails from his inbox. Instead he focused on the display of mouth-watering pastries, croissants and muffins in the glass cabinet facing him and his stomach rumbled appreciatively.

To hell with his usual cup of instant black coffee and burnt toast—his typical mismanaged breakfast because he was inevitably in a hurry.

Message to self: *must hire a housekeeper who can cook.* The last one he'd employed had been a dab hand at making beds, cleaning bathrooms and plumping up cushions, but she'd barely been able to boil an egg, let alone cook him breakfast—which was why Drake had fired her. This morning he was definitely in need of more substantial sustenance—especially in view of the task he was about to undertake. But, whatever his feelings about his home town, he would be viewing this visit with his usual detached professional air. At the end of the day he was here to take an unbiased look round. It was a preliminary to starting work with other professionals on the regeneration of an area that had been as tired and broken as an abandoned and rusted lawn-mower ever since he could remember.

At first when he had been approached by a government official to become involved he had baulked at the very idea. His memories of the area hardly fostered fond and sentimental recollections of a happy, carefree childhood that he would be pleased to revisit…anything *but*. The majority of his work was in the private sector, and up until now Drake had been happy to keep it that way. After all, it had made him rich beyond imagining, and thankfully had taken him far away from the pains of his childhood and youth. Yet in the end he'd seen accepting the commission as a cathartic exercise and an opportunity for him to erase a painful part of his past. For as well as regenerating his home town Drake also planned to demolish the house he'd grown up in and build something much more beautiful in its place.

His cruel father was long dead, but this small act would help Drake feel as if he were mentally freeing himself from his father's grasp. Drake could imagine facing his father and saying to the man, *No matter what you did to me when I was a kid, your despicable treatment is not going to rule the rest of my life. Now I'm the one who's in control, and I'm going to knock this godforsaken house down and erect something in its place that will be testimony to a member of the family that at least has some integrity…who cares about making the environment more beautiful!*

And Drake would do it too. He might have had his issues whilst living there, but nobody could accuse him of being a coward in not facing his demons. To help dissociate the personal from the pragmatic he'd made the decision to treat this commission just as any other architectural project he undertook, and he intended to apply his renowned design skills along with every bit of dedication and experience he had to help make the planned improvements an unmitigated success.

Up until now he'd believed the best way to deal with his sorrowful childhood memories was to relegate them to the deepest, darkest corners of his mind and endeavour to forget about them. It didn't always work, but at least his policy of single-mindedly focusing on what was right in front of him had definitely helped bring rewards beyond even his wildest dreams…

'Good morning. What can I get for you?'

Cutting off his distracted perusal of the goodies inside the display case, Drake glanced up into the most arresting pair of glossy brown eyes he had ever seen. If there were any thoughts in his head at all in that moment he couldn't have said what they were. *He was simply mesmerised.* The owner of those eyes was a girl who was breathtakingly beautiful. She was dressed plainly in a maroon T-shirt with the café's logo on it, and a pair of ordinary blue jeans, with a short navy-coloured apron tied round her trim waist. The nondescript clothing merely emphasised her loveliness.

Her thick dark hair was fashioned into a simple ponytail, and her features were nothing less than sublime. The only evidence of make-up that Drake could detect was the dark eye-pencil that underlined her lower lashes. *How refreshing,* he thought. So many women these days dressed for work as if they were going out to a nightclub. The other thing he noticed about the girl was that she bore a passing resemblance to an Italian movie actress he admired…except she was even prettier.

He was totally unprepared for the dizzying pleasure that assailed him. As his avid gaze met and held hers, he felt as if he was drowning in it. He stared helplessly, just like a dumbfounded schoolboy. 'I'd like a large Americano, a couple of plain croissants—and do you have anything savoury, like a panini?' he asked, his voice a little gruff as he answered because the arresting sight of her had so completely thrown him. 'I'm hungry this morning.'

The girl's big dark eyes widened, as if she was amused, but then she quickly lowered her lashes and looked away. 'We don't have any paninis, but you could have a toasted muffin with some bacon, or even bacon and egg?'

As her glance levelled once more with his, Drake saw her polite smile was definitely guarded. *Had she registered his stunned reaction?* A girl with looks like hers must get men hitting on her all the time. She was probably sick of it. No wonder she seemed wary.

'I'll go for the bacon muffin, I think.'

'Okay.' Her hands were already reaching for a large cream mug and a tray, but her brown eyes met his for another fleeting moment before turning towards the gleaming bank of coffee-making equipment behind her. 'Why don't you take a seat at one of the tables and I'll bring your order over to you?'

'Sure…thanks.'

Drake had immediately noted that the medium-sized cosily proportioned café wasn't exactly teeming with customers on this drizzly September morning. He scanned his surroundings with a bit more attention to detail. The décor, with fading artistic prints on the walls, was definitely a little tired, but there were some charming extras—such as comfy sofas scattered with ethnic print cushions and a bookshelf full of well-thumbed books—which helped create a welcoming and friendly atmosphere. Another plus was that everything appeared scrupulously clean and tidy. But for a café that had a prime location on the high street he knew it ought to be a lot busier than it was to make a profit. Also, the prices he'd seen on the menu were far too low. The owner obviously didn't have a business brain.

He frowned, feeling oddly guilty all of a sudden. Clearly the area had not prospered over the years. Drake was struck anew at how fortunate he was to have escaped the poverty that many of the local population were crippled by, and it certainly wasn't going to get any easier for people in the current economic climate, he knew. At any rate, because the place was so quiet it meant he had his pick of the most appealing tables and the inviting sofas. Selecting a corner seat, he pushed his fingers through his light brown hair and found his attention once again drawn to the beautiful young waitress. The graceful way her slender body moved as she went about preparing his order put him in mind of watching a captivating butterfly.

In the midst of the wistful thought, a wave of irritation assailed him. Usually *nothing* tore him away from his work, but right now the compulsion to focus solely on *her* was doing a good job of exactly that. Consequently, the plans of the area that he'd received from the local council didn't immediately get plucked from his briefcase. Instead he scanned the copy of the *Financial Times* that his chauffeur Jimmy had so thoughtfully handed to him as he'd left the car, but every now and again his glance was helplessly lured back to the girl.

Due to his success as one of the most in-demand architects in the country, Drake had never been bereft of interested female attention. But it had been six months now since Kirsty—his party-planner girlfriend of just under a year—had broken up with him, calling him 'spectacularly selfish' and too work-obsessed to fulfil her hoped-for dreams of marriage and children. *He hadn't denied the accusation.* Frankly, he'd been surprised they'd lasted as long as they had. Usually his relationships didn't extend beyond three to four months.

The truth was, Drake wasn't interested in a deeper commitment. He much preferred having his freedom. The only problem with that was the fact he had a very healthy libido, and wasn't keen on soulless encounters purely for sex. His ex and he hadn't been a match made in heaven, but he had definitely missed having a warm and willing woman in his bed for the past six months…

'Here you are.' The brunette stunner who had prepared his breakfast flashed him another wary smile as she placed his coffee and food down on the table. 'Enjoy,' she added, clearly intent on returning to her post as quickly as possible rather than linger and pass the time of day with him.

'What's your name?' The question was out before Drake could check it.

Her slim shoulders tensed visibly. 'Why?'

Her guarded, less than warm response didn't faze him. He shrugged a shoulder. 'Because I'm curious.'

Turning the tables on him, she challenged, 'What's *your* name?'

'Drake.'

'Is that your first name or your last?'

'My full name is Drake Ashton.'

'Of *course*.' Her widened brown eyes reflected dawning realisation. 'You're the celebrated architect who's going to rejuvenate the area by creating attractive and affordable housing for potentially interested residents.'

She could have tagged *supposedly* onto the end of that sentence, because her tone suggested she doubted that he would be able to do any such thing. Drake was suddenly uncomfortably irked. 'Not by myself…there are other people involved.'

'But if the local papers are anything to go by *you're* the one that's excited all the interest.' She frowned, staring back at him with disturbing candour. 'Home town boy made good…that's the story they're running.'

Straightening his back against the red faux leather seat, he met her examining glance with one equally unflinching and frank. 'Is it? Then seeing as I was born here I guess that more than qualifies me to have an interest in the place…wouldn't you agree, Miss…?' He tipped his head, scanning her well-fitting T-shirt for a badge with her name on it, and not immediately tearing his gaze away when he saw that there wasn't one because the lovely shape of her firm, high breasts outlined by her clothing distracted him disturbingly.

'It's hardly any of my business what your motivations for coming back here are. I apologise if you think I was rude.' Colouring slightly, she shrugged. 'I'm sorry but I have to get back to work now.'

'You still haven't told me your name. And, in case you hadn't noticed, including myself there are only three customers in the whole place. You're not exactly rushed off your feet this morning,' Drake observed wryly, glancing round.

Her cheeks reddened again, but whether this was due to embarrassment or irritation with him for being so persistent, he couldn't tell.

'My name's Layla Jerome, and whether it looks busy or not I have to get back to work. I don't just make drinks and serve them,' she retorted, crossing her arms defensively over her chest. 'There's a myriad of jobs that need to be done in a café. You said you were hungry. You'd better drink your coffee and eat your bacon muffin before they go cold.' And without further ado she marched back behind the counter, looking unashamedly relieved when a female customer with a small child in tow came in.

Layla... The beautiful name certainly suited her exotic good-looks, Drake reflected with satisfaction. Smiling to himself, he raised his mug of coffee to his lips, then reached for the temptingly aromatic muffin on his side plate. Before he left the café he fully intended to get her phone number, and when he did it would become a much better day altogether than he'd been anticipating...

The three other customers besides Drake Ashton—including the young woman and her child—had been and gone, and still the man sat there, absorbed in what appeared to be architectural plans. Layla knew this because he'd signalled to her to come over so that he could order another large Americano. She'd breathed more easily when he hadn't tried to engage her in conversation but simply continued perusing the technical drawings he'd spread out on the table, yet the seductive waft of his expensive sandalwood cologne *did* disturb her. Its potent woody notes had hit her straight in the solar plexus when she'd returned to take his order, making her feel ever so slightly light-headed.

The other thing that had unsettled her was the vaguely amused glance from his curiously light grey eyes when she'd delivered his coffee. Why do that? she thought crossly. *Did he think she was some easily impressed featherbrain who would fall at his feet simply because he smiled at her?* It bothered her that she'd wasted even a second mulling it over—especially when she ought to know better. Her experience of men like him—confident, handsome, *rich* men, who took it as their God-given right to say what they wanted to women like her—had not helped Layla feel remotely easy in their company, and neither did she trust them.

Unfortunately she'd reached that conclusion the hard way. It was why she had given up her prestigious job as PA to an ambitious but unscrupulous broker in the City and returned home to work for her brother Marc in his café instead. Her income had plunged dramatically, but it was worth it to live the much more pared-down and uncomplicated life she lived now. No more paying rent on a London studio apartment that was not much bigger than a utility closet, and no more extortionate dry cleaning bills for the suits, skirts and jackets that her ambitious boss had required her to wear to present the efficient corporate image that he insisted best represented him.

Her change of job and income had also meant the end of expensive lunches in fashionable restaurants with colleagues eager to be seen in all the right places and hopefully headhunted by rival prestigious firms so that they could step up a rung or two on the career ladder. But for Layla the best thing of all about leaving her London life behind was that at least now she was working for someone she trusted. And in return her brother Marc respected and valued *her*—unlike her lying boss, who had fleeced her of all her savings with the promise of a money-making opportunity that would set her up for life. *It hadn't.*

Instead the supposedly failsafe deal had cost her every penny of her hard-earned cash. Although she took full responsibility for allowing her desperation to quit a job she'd grown to hate to make her take such a risky gamble with her savings, she didn't intend to allow herself ever to act so desperately again.

Releasing a long, heartfelt sigh, she let her glance settle on the still preoccupied Drake Ashton. His dark head was bent over the drawings and he was chewing the end of a pencil as he studied them. The picture he made called to mind a small boy mulling over his homework. The wave of compassion that swept through Layla at the idea took her by surprise. The polished handsome architect was surely the last man on earth who needed anyone's compassion!

Her thoughts ran on. She wondered if by visiting her brother's simple little café he had some idea of presenting a much more down to earth image than he was usually purported to have?

The local newspaper stated that he had a tough reputation and took no prisoners. It also said that he lived in a house worth millions in Mayfair, as well as owning property in the South of France and Milan, and that he had made his fortune by designing luxurious homes for the rich and famous. No doubt he was used to taking his morning coffee in locations far more affluent and glamorous than here.

Layla swept her hand irritably down over her ponytail. Why should she care where the man usually drank his coffee? What *did* concern her was that he might report back to the council and his other sponsors that their little café was dreary and rundown and, judging by the woeful lack of customers, would it matter if it had to be closed down to make way for a much more viable business?

The idea stirred white-hot fury in her belly, quickly followed by sickening fear. The café meant everything to her brother Marc. If he got wind that Layla had been less than welcoming to the well-known architect, and had potentially sabotaged his chances for investment because she was still smarting from her bad experience with her ex-boss, it was understandable that he would be furious with her.

An uncomfortable flurry of guilt and regret besieged her insides. The government representatives and council members who had headed up the public meetings she and Marc had attended to hear about the intended plans for the town's regeneration had emphasised that everyone should be as helpful as possible to the influx of professionals who would be working hard on their behalf. Well, one thing was for sure... She hadn't exactly got off to an impressive start with the head architect. Was there the remotest chance she could make a better impression without compromising herself? she wondered.

'Layla?'

She almost jumped out of her skin when the man himself called her over again. Her heart thudded hard. Wiping the back of her hand across suddenly dry lips, she presented herself at Drake Ashton's table. 'Would you like some more coffee?' Along with her bright and friendly smile, she ensured her tone was ultra-polite.

His disturbingly frank grey eyes all but pinned her to the spot. 'Two cups at breakfast is my limit, I'm afraid, else I'll be too wired to think straight. So, no...I don't want any more coffee. Could you sit down for a minute? I'd like to talk to you.'

Swallowing hard, Layla panicked a little. Despite her musings about making a better impression, her gaze automatically sought out an escape route...an incoming customer, perhaps, or even her brother Marc returning from his trip to the suppliers? *But no such luck.* 'What if a customer comes in? You know I'm supposed to be working.'

'You can give me a couple of minutes of your time, surely? If you get a customer then of course you must go and serve them, but right now it's quiet. I want to ask your views about something.'

'Oh, yes?'

'Sit down, Layla...*please.* Hovering makes me uneasy. Did you by any chance fill in one of the questionnaires the council sent round to locals?'

Her relief was palpable. He wanted to ask her about the regeneration of the town, that was all... Nothing more threatening or disturbing than that.

Lowering herself into the chair opposite him, she folded her hands neatly in her lap. 'Yes, I did.'

'Good. Would you mind sharing with me what your views are on the question, "What improvements do you think are most needed in the community"?'

The handsome face before her, with its chiselled jaw and high-sculpted cheekbones, suddenly looked very businesslike and serious. Layla wasn't fazed. This was a topic that she took seriously too. 'Aren't you mainly concerned with designing new housing?'

'I am. But my brief is fairly wide. I've been asked to look at not just housing for potential new residents, but also at what other builds might be possible that would benefit the community in general.'

Curling some hair that had come adrift from her ponytail behind her ear, Layla automatically leaned forward. 'That's music to my ears, because in my opinion one of the things that's most needed in this community is more facilities for the young—by that I mean specifically for teenagers. The reason why a lot of teenagers hang around on street corners with their friends and get into trouble is because there's nowhere for them to go and socialise. They're too young to go to the pub and hang out there, and frankly they don't need another excuse to drink when booze is already sold frighteningly cheaply at supermarkets and already causes havoc. No… What they need is a place specifically for *them*.

'The local so-called "community" hall prides itself on keeping them away. The people who run it won't take the time to get to know any of these kids and find out what they're really like, but they're very quick to judge and demonise them. A place where they can go and listen to music together, maybe play snooker or pool, would be fantastic. We could ask for volunteers from the community to help run it. That way it would bring young and older people together and would benefit us all.'

'You sound like quite the crusader.'

'I make no apology about that. It's great that there are so many campaigns to help the elderly, it really is…but the young need help too. Don't you think?'

Remembering his own emotionally impoverished and lonely childhood, when he had often yearned for somewhere to go where he could just be himself and forget about his unhappy home-life, Drake undoubtedly agreed. Layla's impassioned tone as she had voiced her opinions had taken him aback, made him regard her in a whole new light. *It had also strengthened his vow to get her phone number.* In his world he didn't often meet people who cared half as much about the welfare of others, and it certainly didn't hurt that she was beautiful too…

'I agree,' he commented thoughtfully. 'I'm going to look over some plots in the next few days for potential new builds, and I'll definitely bear in mind what you've told me. Of course I can make recommendations, but ultimately the decision to establish a youth club or something similar lies with the council. They're the ones who'll have to allocate the funds.'

'I know that. But an important man like you…' Her eyes shone with renewed zeal. 'A man who grew up in the area himself…perhaps you could bring some of your influence to bear? It would mean such a lot to the kids if you could.'

They both glanced towards the door as it swung

open, heralding the entrance of a frail-looking elderly couple.

'Looks like you've got some customers.' Drake smiled, but his lovely companion was already on her feet and making her way back behind the counter.

Half an hour later Layla noticed that Drake was folding up the plans into a stylish leather briefcase. She chewed down on her lip as he crossed the room to speak to her. It felt as if every sense she had was on high alert as he neared. The man was seriously imposing, she realised. The shoulders beneath his stylish jacket were athletically broad, and his lean, muscular build and long legs meant that he would look good in whatever he wore—whether it was the dark grey chinos and smart blue shirt he was wearing now, or a scruffy pair of jeans and a T-shirt. Suddenly she seemed to be preternaturally aware of everything about him. He moved as if he owned the space and everything in it. And the amused, knowing glint in his silvery grey eyes made her stomach coil with tension.

'The coffee and food were great—particularly the coffee,' he commented, setting his briefcase down on the floor.

'I'm glad you enjoyed it. My brother, who owns the café, buys the very best grade coffee he can get his hands on, and he took great pride in teaching me how to make it. His aim is always to deliver a good product and good service to his customers.'

'In business that's one of the best intentions you can have…that and being dedicated to making a profit. I meant to ask you before who owned the place. So it's your brother? What's his name?'

'Marc Jerome.'

Her questioner tunnelled his long, artistic fingers through his hair, unwittingly drawing her attention to his strong, indomitable-looking brow. There were two deeply ingrained furrows there, she saw.

'Have you always worked for him?' he asked.

'No.' An unconscious sigh left her lips. 'Not always.'

Drake looked bemused. 'You don't care to embellish on that?'

'I worked in London for a few years, but I needed a change so I—I came back home.' Lifting her chin a little, Layla wrestled with her usual reluctance to reveal much more than that.

'What did you do in London?'

'I was a personal assistant to a broker in the City.'

Raising a quizzical eyebrow, Drake looked even more bemused. 'This is quite a career change for you, then?'

'Yes, it is. Is there anything else you want to ask me before I get back to work, Mr Ashton?'

'Yes.' His gaze suddenly became disturbingly intense. 'There *is* something else, Layla. I'd like your telephone number.'

'Why?'

'So that I can ring you and invite you out for a drink. Will you give it to me?'

Shock eddied through her like an ice-cold river. She hadn't missed the gleam of admiration in his eyes when he'd first seen her, but she hadn't expected him to invite her out or to be quite so quick in asking for her phone number.

'If you'd asked for my brother's number, so you could

talk to him about his views on the area's regeneration or about his business, then I would have been more than happy to give it to you. But to be honest I'm not in the habit of giving my number to men I hardly know.'

'But you *do* know who I am. By that I mean I'm not some stranger who's just walked in off the street. And, whilst I would definitely appreciate having your brother's number so that I can ask him a few questions, right now it's *yours* that I'm far more interested in.'

'I'm sorry.' Uncomfortably twisting her hands together, she nonetheless made herself meet his intense silvery gaze unflinchingly. 'My answer is still no. I enjoyed our little chat earlier about what's needed in the community, and I'm very encouraged by your interest, but—well…let's just leave it at that, shall we?' The need to protect herself from another over-confident and arrogant wealthy man like her ex-boss was definitely at the forefront of her mind as she spoke.

With a sigh, Drake stretched his sculpted lips into a slow, knowing smile 'Maybe we will and maybe we *won't*…leave it at that, I mean.'

He didn't sound at all offended. In fact, as he picked up his briefcase, he gave her another enigmatic glance.

'This is hardly the busiest or most populated town in the country. No doubt we'll bump into each other from time to time. In fact I'm certain we will. Have a good day, won't you? Oh—and why don't you give your brother my number? I'd very much like to have a chat with him about his views on the town.'

He slid the business card that he'd taken from his jacket pocket across the counter, not waiting to see if she picked it up to examine it.

Opening the heavy glass door, he stepped outside onto the damp and grey pavement, and as Layla watched him go several seconds passed before she realised she was holding her breath…

CHAPTER TWO

JEROME... The name should have rung a bell as soon as he heard it. Slowing his stride, Drake turned his head to take another look at the faded, worn exterior of the building he'd just vacated. As soon as Layla had given him her surname he ought to have remembered that it was the name of the newsagents that had been in business there before the café. The place had been called Jerome's, for goodness' sake. Had the friendly newsagent who had often discussed the football results with him while he was waiting for his dad to make up his mind about what he wanted been her father? he wondered.

Drake calculated that she must be at least ten years younger than he was. That put her age at about twenty-six. He wondered whether, if he mentioned to Layla that he'd had genuine regard for her father, it might help persuade her to meet him for a drink—better still, dinner. At any rate, unless she had a boyfriend he wasn't going to give up on the idea any time soon. Not when his first sight of her had been akin to falling into a dream he didn't want to wake up from. He'd felt stunned, dazed and disorientated all at once, and it was hard to recall the last time his heart had galloped so hard and so fast.

It struck him that she was the first woman who had ever declined to give him her phone number. *It made him all the more determined to get her to change her mind.*

Shaking his head in a bid to snap out of his reverie about the beautiful waitress, he determinedly walked on further down the street, stopping every now and then to make notes on his observations about the buildings and the retail outlets that occupied them. When he'd travelled about halfway down the road Drake's finely honed instincts alerted him to the fact that he was being followed. Turning, he saw two men that were clearly from the press. It was pointless trying to fathom how they'd known he would be there. Somehow or other they always found out.

One of them was toting a state-of-the-art camera and the other a recording device. He just thanked his lucky stars the pair hadn't invaded the café to try and interview him or he wouldn't have had much conversation with the lovely Layla at all. Because they hadn't, he was predisposed to be a lot less irritated with them than was usually the case when the press unexpectedly cornered him.

'We're from the local newspaper, Mr Ashton. Can we have a picture and maybe a quick interview with you for our readers? As you can imagine, everyone is very excited about your intended rehabilitation of the area and what the social and economic effects might be.' The journalist with the recording equipment planted himself directly in front of Drake with an animated smile.

'Okay. But the interview had better be quick because I've got work to do.'

'Of course, Mr Ashton, but if we could just have a couple of pictures first that would be great.'

He tolerated the photos being taken, and then an interview, with an uncharacteristically amenable attitude—even when a small knot of curious bystanders gathered to see what was going on. The questions had been surprisingly intelligent and insightful, despite the apparent youth of the reporter, but when he had asked, 'Can you tell us a bit about your personal experience of growing up here?' it had been one question too far.

Drake had called an abrupt halt to the exchange, and phoned his chauffeur Jimmy and instructed him to meet him at the top of the high street. His heart was still racing uncomfortably as he turned his back on the journalist, photographer and bystanders and walked briskly away.

He was seriously relieved to see the sleek Aston Martin coming down the road towards him. Now he could focus on his work without impediment. There were a few other areas in the locality he wanted to survey before attending a meeting at the town hall to make a brief report, but after that he would be returning to his offices in London to oversee a couple of prestigious projects that were nearing completion. Projects that, although adding substantially to his bank balance and growing reputation, had been far trickier and more time-consuming than he'd anticipated, consequently causing him more troubled nights of broken sleep than he cared to recall…

'So, what was your impression of Drake Ashton when you met him?'

Her brother had invited Layla downstairs to have

some fish and chips with him that evening. After inheriting the family home in their dad's will, they'd agreed to split the accommodation between them rather than sell it, and had had the two floors converted into self-contained separate flats. Layla had the upper floor and Marc the lower. When she'd moved to London—even though she'd suggested that he rent out her flat while she was gone—Marc had insisted he wouldn't even think of it because it was her home. It would remain unoccupied until she returned, he'd declared, whether that was in one year or ten, and in the meantime she could come home for the odd weekend to see him.

When her career had come to its unexpectedly ignominious and humiliating end because of her crooked boss she'd been very grateful that she had a place to return to where she felt safe again. Being swindled out of her savings had left her feeling vulnerable and unsure of herself, and she hadn't minded admitting to her brother that she needed to retreat from city life for a while to rebuild her confidence. Marc had responded by lovingly welcoming her home without judgement and giving her a job in his café.

Now, as Layla busied herself sorting out condiments and cutlery, Marc unwrapped the fish and chips he'd bought and expertly arranged the food on the plates he'd left warming in the oven. He was looking especially tired tonight, Layla noticed. There were dark rings under his eyes, and with his brown hair clearly not combed and his lean jaw unshaven he was looking a little the worse for wear. *Had he been worrying about money again?* Her heart bumped guiltily beneath her ribs at the mere idea. She knew that the council tax on the business premises had just gone up again, and the café's takings were already substantially below what they would normally expect this month. The recession had hit all the local businesses hard.

'What was my impression?' she hedged, thinking hard about what to say and what *not* to say about her encounter with the charismatic architect. The experience had been on her mind a little *too* much that day, and she wished it hadn't. 'He looks like a man who knows exactly what he wants and how to get it. By that I mean you can tell why he's been so successful. He was very businesslike and focused. I get the impression that very little gets past him.'

'Let's sit down at the table and eat, shall we?' Marc forked a couple of mouthfuls of food into his mouth and swallowed it down before lifting his head to look directly at his sister. 'They say he's an investor as well as an architect. Did you know that?'

'No, I didn't.'

'I'd really like to talk to him about the café.'

'You mean ask his advice on how to help make it more financially viable?'

'Not just that. I want to ask whether he'd be interested in investing in it.' Exhaling a harsh breath, he wiped his napkin irritably across his mouth, then scrunched it into a ball.

Alarmed, Layla laid down her fork beside her plate and stared at him. 'Are we in trouble?'

'We're operating at a serious loss. How could we not be? Trying to attract more customers when everyone around here is so fearful of spending money on anything but the bare necessities is like trying to get blood out of a stone! I've had two loans so far from the bank to help keep it going, and I'm in debt to the tune of several thousand pounds. I've invested all the money Dad left me to start it up and get it going, and now it looks like I might even lose the premises that he worked so hard to own. The café needs a serious injection of something, Layla, or else we're just going to have to throw in the towel.'

Layla would do anything to help her brother feel more optimistic about the café—his *pride and joy* as he'd called it when he'd first decided to set it up. It made her heart feel bruised to see him looking so tired and worried all the time. But his intention to ask Drake Ashton to invest in it scared the life out of her. The man might be admired in his field, and have a glamorous professional profile, but they had no idea what his character or his values were.

Silently she berated herself again for trusting her own life savings to a money-making scheme that—with hindsight—had had so many holes in it. It was a wonder her boss hadn't handed out life rafts to the gullible fools who had risked their hard-earned cash in it! If she'd held onto her money she could have given it to Marc to pay off his bank loan, and straight away ease his fear and worry about the café's future.

Brushing back her hair with her fingers, she emitted a gentle, resigned sigh. 'He gave me his business card to give to you,' she told him. 'He said he'd like to talk to you.'

'Drake Ashton wants to talk to *me*?' Straight away Marc's dark eyes gleamed with hope.

Layla nibbled anxiously at her lip. 'He's an astute

businessman, Marc, and from what you say the café is losing money hand over fist. I don't get the impression that he'd be in a hurry to invest his money in a concern that doesn't have the potential to make a healthy profit.'

'Thanks for your support.'

At his stricken expression she reached forward and squeezed his hand. 'You know my support and belief in you are unquestionable, and I think the café is wonderful...I just wish more people did too. I don't want you to build your hopes up that Drake Ashton might be the answer to your prayers, that's all. We might have to think of other options other than investment...that's all I'm saying.'

'You're right.' Pulling his hand away from hers, Marc lightly shook his head and smiled. 'Trouble is I let my heart rule my head too much. I realise that's not the best approach to running a business. Wanting a thing to work so much that it makes your ribs ache just thinking about it doesn't necessarily mean it's suddenly going to take flight and make your fortune. But it's worth talking to Ashton anyway...he might give me a few tips at least. Give me his card in the morning and I'll ring him. In the meantime let's eat, shall we? Our supper's going cold.'

Layla smiled, but inside she secretly prayed that when they spoke Drake Ashton wouldn't thoughtlessly crush her brother's dream into the dirt by telling him he should forget about the café and think about doing something else instead...

Turning his head, Drake squinted at the sunlight streaming in through the huge plate-glass windows. The hexagon-shaped chrome and glass building that housed his offices had become quite a landmark amid the sea of sandblasted Victorian buildings where it was situated, and he was justifiably proud of the design. If he'd wanted to shout out his arrival he couldn't have made a bolder or louder statement. His workplace was a professional portfolio all by itself.

When the thought sneaked up on him from time to time that what he'd achieved was nothing less than a miracle, considering his background, he impatiently brushed it away, not caring to dwell on the past for even a second longer than he had to. It had become his motto to concentrate on the now. After all, the present made far more sense to him than the past could ever do.

'Mr Ashton? There's a man called Marc Jerome on the phone. He says you gave your business card to his sister so that he could call you.'

Drake's secretary Monica appeared in the doorway to his office. She was a pencil-slim blonde whose efficiency and dedication to her job belied her delicate appearance. The woman could be a veritable tiger when it came to sifting out and diverting unwanted callers—whether on the phone or if they turned up unannounced. But the knowledge that it was Layla Jerome's brother who was ringing made Drake immediately anxious to take the call. The beautiful woman had been almost constantly on his mind ever since he'd seen her, and if nothing else he wasn't going to miss the opportunity to try and get her phone number again.

'Put him through, Monica. I'll take it.'

At the end of the call Drake pushed to his feet and moved restlessly across to the tall plate-glass panels directly behind his desk. Staring out at the parked cars on the street below, he could barely suppress the gratifying sense of satisfaction that throbbed through him. He had listened to Marc Jerome's views on the needs of his local community, and when the younger man had asked for some business tips he had agreed to meet up with him so that they could discuss it more fully.

When that topic was safely out of the way Drake hadn't been slow to seize the opportunity to ask directly if his sister was currently dating anyone. He had all but held his breath as he'd waited for the answer.

'No, she's not,' Marc had replied carefully, definitely sounding protective. 'As far as I know, she's quite happy being free and single right now.'

Drake had allowed himself the briefest smile. 'I'd really like to ask her about that myself, if you don't mind?' he'd returned immediately. There was a fine line between being bold enough to state your aim clearly and being pushy, but when it came to something he wanted as badly as this, he definitely wasn't a man to let the grass grow under his feet—and neither was he overly concerned if he offended anyone. 'It's probably best if I talk to her outside of work. Maybe even on the day that you and I have our meeting?'

'You'd better ring her first and check and see if that's okay,' had been the distinctly wary-sounding reply.

'Of course.'

And now Layla's mobile phone number was writ large across his notepad.

He made a vow to ring her after lunch, just in case the café was busy, and, breathing out a relieved sigh, stopped gazing out the window and returned to his desk, bringing his focus determinedly back to his work...

'Layla?'

'Yes?'

'This is Drake Ashton. I got your number from your brother Marc.'

In the midst of a leisurely stroll in the park, through the sea of burnished gold leaves that scattered the concrete path, Layla changed direction and strode across the grass to sit down on a nearby bench and take the call, her phone positioned firmly against her ear. Marc had despatched her to eat her packed lunch and get some fresh air after a surprising flurry of lunchtime trade, but any sense of feeling free to enjoy a precious hour in the autumnal sunshine had immediately vanished at the sound of the famed architect's magnetically velvet smoky voice.

'He told me you'd asked him for my number,' she answered, already desperately rehearsing her carefully worded refusal of what she suspected would be another invitation to meet him for a drink.

Inexplicably, and against every impulse to act sensibly, she'd hardly been able to stop thinking about the man since he'd visited the café yesterday, and that was definitely a cause for concern. Just hearing his voice ignited an almost terrifying compulsion to see him again. The ethereal grey eyes that sometimes seemed almost colourless, the high cheekbones and cut-glass jaw seemed to be imprinted on her memory with pin-sharp clarity.

'Then you'll no doubt have guessed that I'm ringing to ask you out?' There was a smile in his extraordinarily hypnotic voice. 'I know you were reluctant to let me have your number, but I'd very much like to see you again. I'd really like the chance to get to know you a little, Layla. What do you say?'

'If I'm honest, I'm not entirely comfortable with the idea, Mr Ashton.'

'Drake,' he inserted smoothly.

The tension in Layla's stomach made her feel as if a band of steel was encircling it and tightening by the second. She drew the canvas bag that contained her sandwiches more closely to her side almost subconsciously, as if for protection. 'I don't mean to offend you, but I'm not interested in seeing anyone at the moment.'

'You don't like dating?'

'I can take it or leave it, to tell you the truth. I'm certainly not a person who needs to have someone special in my life to make me feel whole or worthwhile.'

'Good for you. But is that the *real* reason you're hesitating to meet me, or is it perhaps because your last boyfriend let you down in some way or treated you badly?'

'That's none of your business.'

'Maybe not. I'm just trying to find out why you don't want to have a date with me.'

Layla expelled a heavy, resigned sigh. 'The man who let me down wasn't a boyfriend…at least not at first. But he *was* someone I'd put my trust in—completely wrongly, as it turned out. I was very badly deceived by him. Anyway, I—'

'You'd rather not risk seeing me in case I do the same thing to you?' Drake finished for her.

'No, I'd rather not,' she confessed reluctantly, feeling strangely as though she'd manoeuvred herself into a narrow dead-end she couldn't easily reverse out of.

'Not all men are bastards, Layla.'

'I know that. I'd trust my brother Marc with my life.'

'Speaking of your family—I knew your father, you know?'

Her heartbeat quickened in surprise. 'Really?'

'Jerome's was my local newsagent. That's where I knew him from.'

'It's a small world.'

'I used to go there as a kid. We'd chat about football together. We supported the same team, and he used to tell me about all the matches he'd seen when he was young.'

'He was crazy about football. And he loved having the opportunity to talk to another fan about the game— also about how his team were doing. My dad always had time for the children who visited the shop. He had the kindest heart.' Suddenly besieged by memories of the father she had adored, as well as by a great longing for his physical presence, Layla couldn't help the tears that suddenly surged into her eyes.

'Presumably he's not around any more? What happened, if you don't mind my asking?'

'He died just three months after a diagnosis of cancer of the throat.'

'I'm sorry. That must have been a very hard cross to bear for you and your brother.'

'It was.'

'And your mother? Is she still around?'

'She died when I was nine. Look, Mr Ashton, I—'

'I'd really like it if you called me Drake.'

The invitation sounded so seductively appealing that even though she intuited that he'd used his past association with her father to break down her resistance, Layla found his skilful persuasion hard to ignore. Although her trust in men had been indisputably shattered by the dishonest behaviour of her boss, Drake's regard for her father seemed perfectly genuine, she told herself.

Her lips edged helplessly into a smile. 'You don't give up easily, do you?'

'No, I don't. You don't get far in the world of business if you're not tenacious.'

'I hear that you've agreed to meet with my brother and give him some advice about the café?'

'I'm coming to see him on Thursday. After our meeting at the café I'm visiting the site where the first new builds for residential housing are going to be erected. I expect I'll be there until quite late.'

Not knowing what to say, Layla shivered at the icy blast of wind that suddenly tore through her hair and swept the leaves on the path into a mini-cyclone.

'Look…I really want to see you,' he asserted, 'but I don't want to wait until Thursday. That's far too long.' He made no attempt to disguise his impatience. 'How about throwing any caution you might be harbouring to the wind and going on just one date with me? If you come up to London I'll take you out to dinner.'

'When were you thinking of?'

'Tomorrow… No, wait! *Tonight*…I want to see you tonight.'

'Tonight is a bit short notice.'

Her inner guidance was already sending a loud warning to be careful pounding through her bloodstream.

When her brother had confessed that he'd given Drake her number she hadn't been able to help feeling annoyed at *both* men. She wasn't some desirable commodity to be bartered over, for goodness' sake! Neither had she expected the architect to ring her so soon. She'd like more time to mull his invitation over…*time to come to her senses, more like,* she thought irritably. Her ex-boss had had a way with words too, and had been a master at devising clever strategies to get what he wanted— sometimes underhand ones. She shouldn't forget that. Although when it came to sheer charisma she didn't doubt that Drake Ashton easily had the market cornered.

'Have you other plans for tonight?'

'No, but tomorrow night would suit me better.' Hardly knowing where she'd found the nerve to tell him that, Layla grimaced.

'I might not be able to make it tomorrow night.'

'Never mind.' Holding on to her determination not to be railroaded into flying off to London at the drop of a hat simply because Drake demanded it, she shook her head. 'It will have to be Thursday after all, then.' She deliberately kept her tone matter-of-fact. The other end of the line went ominously quiet. 'Are you still there, Drake?'

His sharp intake of breath was followed by an equally audible sigh of frustration and her insides knotted.

'I'm still here.' Irritation was evident in every sylla- ble. 'Tomorrow night it is, then. Give me your address and I'll send my driver to pick you up and bring you to my office. It's close to the West End, and I'll book us somewhere nice for dinner.'

'You don't have to send your driver. I can easily get the train into London.'

'Are you always this bull-headed?'

Even though Drake was probably still irked with her for trying to thwart him, disconcertingly he chuckled, and the husky sound sent shivers cascading up and down her spine like sparks from a firework.

'Because if you are, Layla, then I think I might have just met my match…'

CHAPTER THREE

SHE was half an hour late.

Having already been into his secretary's office twice to see if Layla had left a message, Drake now found himself in front of the coffee machine on the landing outside his office, pressing the button for yet another cup of strong black Americano he didn't really want.

Time had moved through the day like silt through reeds—slowly and painfully and laboriously, going nowhere fast. Whenever he thought about seeing Layla his insides were seized by alternate sensations of excitement and disagreeable anxiety. And several times that day a couple of colleagues had enquired if anything was wrong.

He hated the idea that they could see he was unsettled by something. Usually he endeavoured to keep his feelings strictly to himself—sometimes to the point of unsettling *them* because he expressed none of the usual emotional 'ups and downs' as they did. Yet he was quick to sing their praises when they did a good job for him, or worked overtime to help meet a deadline. Having built his reputation not on just designing builds to wow his clients but also by advising on and overseeing a project right up until the finish, Drake had ensured the people

he employed were trustworthy and reliable team play-
ers. He might have grown up the quintessential 'loner'
but he couldn't do what he did without them.

Glancing down at his watch, it jolted him to see the
time. *Damn it all to hell!* Why hadn't he insisted that
Layla let him send Jimmy to collect her instead of allowing her to make her own way here? He hadn't because he'd got the feeling if he had she would have
cancelled their date altogether and told him just to forget it…

'Your visitor has arrived, Mr Ashton.'

The quiet, knowing tone of Monica, his secretary,
broke into his unhappy reverie. To his dismay, he knew
she'd guessed that the woman he was waiting to see
was no run-of-the-mill visitor…that she was in some
way special. If he quizzed her she'd call this instinct
women's intuition, and Drake couldn't for the life of
him understand why women had the gift in abundance
and men didn't. At any rate, he intensely disliked people expressing curiosity or interest in his private life—
and that included *unspoken* interest.

Monica's announcement that Layla had arrived had
him turning towards her so fast that the scalding coffee in his polystyrene cup splashed painfully onto his
hand. He uttered a furious expletive.

The secretary's smile was replaced by an immediately concerned frown. 'You'd better get some cold
water on that straight away,' she advised urgently, stepping towards him to relieve him of the cup.

'Where have you put her?' Drake barked, the sting of
his scald aiding neither his temper nor his impatience.

'In your office.'

'Well, make sure she's comfortable and tell her I'll be there in a couple of minutes. I'm going to the bathroom to run some cold water over my hand.'

Staring at his reflection in the mirror over the sink, and not particularly liking what he saw, Drake scrubbed his hand over the five o'clock stubble that darkened his jaw and ignored the throb of his burn with stoic indifference. Knowing he was going out to dinner, he ought to have shaved—but it was too late now. His date would just have to take him as she found him, even though he more closely resembled a dishevelled croupier who'd been up all night rather than a successful and wealthy architect. At least he was wearing one of his hand-tailored suits, with a silk waistcoat over a white open-necked shirt. That should help him pass muster.

Muttering out loud at the agitation that rendered him nowhere *near* relaxed, he straightened his shirt collar and spun away from the mirror. He refused to put himself through the grinder about anything else tonight. Work was finished for the day and he was going out to dinner with a woman who had rendered him dangerously fascinated the instant his gaze had fallen into hers…

As he made his way back to his office an older colleague attempted to waylay him with a query. Drake was so intent on seeing Layla that he stared at the man as if suddenly confronted by a ghost.

'Ask me about it tomorrow,' he muttered distractedly. 'I'm busy right now.'

'Sorry if I interrupted something important.'

Looking bemused, his fellow architect exited the glass-partitioned landing and Drake continued on into the executive office suite that was his private domain. Standing outside the semi-open door, he sucked in a steadying breath before making his entry. Just before his gaze alighted on the woman he'd been waiting all day to see his senses picked up the sultry trail of her perfume, and the alluring scent made his blood pound with heat. When his eyes finally rested on the slim dark-haired figure standing by his desk, dressed in a classy cream-coloured wool coat over a black cocktail dress, he could barely hear himself think over the dizzying waves of pleasure that submerged him. His little wait-ress looked like a million dollars.

'You made it,' he said, low-voiced.

'Yes. Though I don't know why I came.'

'What do you mean?'

'I mean that I haven't accepted an invitation to din-ner from a man in a very long time, and I'm still not sure why I accepted yours.'

'Well, I'm glad that you did. You look very beauti-ful tonight, by the way.'

'Thanks.'

His compliment had clearly discomfited her, Drake saw.

'I don't normally dress like this,' she dissembled, 'but I didn't know where we were going so I— Anyway, are you annoyed that I'm late? The tube was delayed in a tunnel for twenty minutes…I don't like to think why. I'm sorry if I kept you waiting.'

'There's no need to apologise. Although I did recom-mend that my driver pick you up rather than you getting the train, remember?'

'*Recommend?* Is that what you did?' Shaking her

head, Layla forgot her previous awkwardness and emitted a throaty chuckle.

Already entranced by her beauty and presence, Drake was all but undone by the sound.

'As I recall,' she continued with a wry smile, 'it sounded more like a royal command. But then I expect you're used to telling people what to do and having it done?'

He kept quiet, because what she said was perfectly true. Yet he didn't want her to gain the impression he was insufferably overbearing and demanding and not give him a chance to display some of the less 'insufferable' sides to his nature... For the first time ever he was suddenly unsure of his ground with a woman. The percentages that afforded him command of any relationship were usually stacked in his favour—sixty-forty at least...

'Anyway, I still can't believe I'm standing here in your office.' Sighing softly, Layla smoothed her hand down over her hair. 'I guessed it would be impressive, but even my imagination didn't stretch as far as a hexagonal glass building that looks like something out of a futuristic sci-fi film. How on earth do you make something like this?'

'A hexagonal building is definitely harder to construct than a square-cornered one, but apart from its unique exterior it makes for a far more interesting interior to live and work in. I'm all for enhancing domestic and business spaces, and hopefully getting people to enjoy spending time in them. Do you like it?'

'All this glass...' She glanced to her right and then to her left, and then up above her at the ceiling and its breathtaking view of the twilit sky. 'It must be so light in here during the day. I definitely like the idea of that.'

'That's why I had the roof made out of glass. Sometimes I work in here at night, and if the moon is full and the stars are out I switch off the lamps for a while because they're not needed. The illumination from the sky is so bright that it's like a shroud of magical light blanketing everything.'

His companion's big brown eyes were so transfixed by what he said that this time it was Drake who was discomfited. He'd never admitted to anyone that he did such a thing before, and certainly not to any of his colleagues. What on earth had possessed him to be so candid?

In a bid to divert Layla from the too personal confession he smiled and said, 'Want me to give you a tour?'

Her smooth cheeks flushed a little. 'Maybe some other time… Aren't we supposed to be going out to dinner?'

'Are you telling me that you're hungry?'

'I am, actually. But the truth is I don't feel at my best in offices—even one as beautiful as this. My experience of being a personal assistant robbed me of all desire to ever work in one again. The world of "shocks and scares"—as my brother Marc calls it—was like a bear pit, and to work in an atmosphere where there's such a high level of drama and tension every day is apt to make a person permanently on edge. It's a lot more peaceful working in the café.'

Intrigued, Drake walked behind his desk and slipped on the tailored black jacket that he'd hung almost thoughtlessly over the back of his chair. It barely registered these days that the cost of his clothing far exceeded most ordinary people's annual salaries. But then if you wanted the best, you had to pay for the best. *He'd come a long way from the boy whose father had dressed him in charity shop finds.*

Frowning at the bewitching girl who stood in front of his desk, he asked, 'Can you tell me what your boss the broker was like?'

'I'd rather not. At least not right now. Perhaps when I get to know you a bit better?'

His heart slammed against his ribs. 'Can I take it, then, that you're planning on us having more than one date?'

'I'm not planning anything…it's a policy of mine to always try and live in the moment.'

'Mine too.'

'Besides…it's not just up to me, is it? Who knows? By the end of the evening you might be glad to see the back of me.'

'Somehow that's not how I envisage the evening ending.' Quirking a droll eyebrow, Drake gestured that they should move towards the door. 'Let's go to dinner, shall we? I've booked us a table at a nice French restaurant I know.'

They had been escorted by an ultra-polite *maître d'* to what Layla imagined must be the best table in the house. The 'nice' French restaurant Drake had mentioned turned out to be one of the most acclaimed eateries in Europe…let alone London. It had two Michelin stars and was populated tonight by an extremely classy-looking clientele who clearly weren't short of a penny or two. Their table was situated in a discreet far corner of the room, and the candlelit setting was quite simply beautiful. Everything from the polished silverware to the gleaming candelabrum and the white linen table-cloth that was hung with frightening precision was ar-ranged to exemplify the most exquisite good taste, and the genteel ambience was further emphasised by some softly playing classical music.

Drake touched his hand lightly to her back as Layla's seat was pulled out for her by the *maître d'*, and he waited until he saw she was comfortable before seating himself. *Was it normal to have felt his touch as strongly as though a powerful electrical current had penetrated her layers of clothing?* God knew she'd been jumpy enough at his office, but alone with him like this, in an intimate setting far away from any working envi-ronment, she feared she would display her unease and self-consciousness by talking far too much. Back at his office she'd already babbled and said more than she'd meant to say. And what on earth had possessed her to suggest she might like to get to know him better? For a woman who had vowed to steer well clear of men of Drake Ashton's elite calibre, she was doing abysmally poorly. Now she was sure that the heat he had ignited in her body with his brief touch must easily be displayed on her burning face.

'I've heard about this place—of course I have—but I never thought I'd be so lucky as to get the chance to eat here. Rumour has it that the waiting list for a table is at least a year long. Is that true, do you think?'

Her restless hands nervously folded and unfolded her

linen napkin. The magnetic silver-grey eyes in front of her glinted with amusement.

'I have no idea. I simply had my secretary ring and book me a table.'

Layla didn't get the chance to comment straight away, because just then a waiter handed them leather-bound menus and a female sommelier appeared to make recommendations for the wine they might like to order. She didn't miss the fact that the attractive and vivacious redhead obviously knew Drake. The woman was completely professional, but she all but lit up when she saw him, and the banter between them sounded as though it was borne of a long-standing association.

When she'd left them alone again Layla sipped at the glass of water another waiter had poured for her and wondered if the sommelier and Drake had ever enjoyed a far closer relationship. *The idea bothered her far more than it had a right to.*

'The reason you have no idea how long the waiting list is for a table,' she announced jerkily, 'is obviously because you're an important man whose name alone gets you an automatic foot in the door.'

'You sound as if that perturbs you.'

Her handsome date narrowed his gaze and she felt as if she'd just voluntarily put herself under a high-powered microscope that would hunt out every flaw and discrepancy in her character and ruthlessly bring it to light.

'Why should it bother you that I can get a table in a good restaurant without having to wait for a similar time as most people do?'

Her skin prickling hotly with embarrassment, Layla frowned, feeling not just guilty and foolish but extremely gauche. 'I didn't mean to suggest that it bothered me. It was really just an observation. You've obviously worked hard to have the privileges you enjoy and I don't even know why I mentioned it. Forgive me. Put it down to nerves.'

'So I make you nervous, do I?'

'Yes, you do a little.'

'Why is that?'

'Maybe you mistakenly think I'm a lot more confident than I am? The truth is I'm just a girl from an ordinary suburban home, and I'm not that comfortable in the company of privileged men like yourself.'

She'd hoped her honest admission might alleviate some of the anxiety she felt around Drake, but it didn't. Instead she was left feeling even more gauche and unsophisticated.

At that very moment the pretty sommelier returned with their wine and proceeded to pour some into Drake's glass for him to taste and approve. When he indicated with a nod of his head that he did indeed approve, she poured some into Layla's. This time her companion's compelling glance didn't remotely invite the girl to linger longer than was absolutely necessary.

'Thank you,' he murmured, his businesslike tone suggesting she should leave. 'Your health and happiness,' he toasted, smiling at Layla.

The gesture was a long way from being businesslike. His captivating eyes crinkled at the corners as he smiled and his lips curved generously, displaying strong white teeth. It was a killer combination and her body tightened helplessly.

'The same to you,' she murmured, lightly touching her goblet-shaped wine glass to his.

'And, by the way, I didn't get the impression that you were especially confident. My general impression is that you're rather defensive, and consequently quite feisty because of it. Like a protective lioness wanting to divert attention away from a predator's interest in her cub.'

'I wasn't trying to protect anyone.'

'Yes, you were.' Drake's rich voice lowered meaningfully. 'You were clearly trying to protect yourself, Layla.'

'Is that so? Then, tell me, exactly what am I protecting myself *from*? I'd be very interested to know.' Inside her chest, Layla's heartbeat mimicked the disturbing cadence of a chugging steam train.

'From *me*.' As he carefully set down his wine glass, still holding onto the fragile stem with his forefinger and thumb, Drake's gleaming intense glance all but devoured her.

'But, saying that, I'm no predator. As far as women are concerned I've never found the need.'

His gaze continued to hold her spellbound, and she was helpless to break free from it.

'I've never had to chase a woman in my life. It's always been the other way round. However...' Again he paused, as if carefully measuring his words. 'I've always guessed that one day there would be an exception to break the rule.'

Feeling as if pure elemental lightning was scorching through her veins, Layla nervously licked her lips, feverishly trying to find coherent words to answer such an incendiary declaration. 'Are you—are you saying that you're pursuing me, Drake?'

His amused, provocative chuckle emanated from deep inside his throat. 'I hope I won't have to, Layla. But I rather think that will be up to you.'

Lifting his glass, he drank deeply from wine that the candlelight on the table seemed to turn into a deeply seductive blood-red river...

'Are you and your guest ready to order, Mr Ashton?'

The waiter's reappearance was well timed. It saved her from having to make a reply to a comment whose repercussions were still imploding shockingly inside her. She wasn't naive as far as men's desires were concerned. Her looks had often invited interested male attention... most of it *unwanted*. But never before had Layla been in a position where a man—a much admired and well-known man—told her so frankly that he would pursue her if she indicated she wasn't interested.

Already she'd discovered that it was near impossible *not* to be interested in Drake. Every moment they spent together she was fighting hard to tamp down the flames of desire his mercurial silver gaze ignited every time his eyes met hers. It was going to be one almighty challenge to resist such an electrifying attraction for long.

At the waiter's polite enquiry Drake opened the menu that had been languishing on the table in front of him, but before scanning it he glanced pointedly at Layla and said, 'I think we need a few more minutes, don't you?'

Not trusting herself to speak right then, she merely nodded her head.

'We need a little more time,' he told the waiter, who

promptly and deferentially blended back into the general hub of the restaurant. 'Shall I pour you some more wine?'

His lovely companion had been silent for the past few minutes as they ate their meal, and whenever Drake found himself helplessly studying her she seemed to be lost in a world of her own. Whilst he didn't particularly mind the lapse in conversation, he was concerned that she might be regretting their date—and that was something he expressly *didn't* want her to do. He should never have admitted so frankly that he would indeed pursue her if she indicated indifference to him. But in that unguarded moment lust and desire had got the better of him and his feelings had been hard to contain.

'No, thanks.' She declined his offer of more wine. 'I can't drink too much tonight. I've got a train to catch, and I've also got to get up early for work in the morning.'

'You don't have to rush to catch a train. My chauffeur will drive you home.'

'How will you get home if your chauffeur drives me?'

Drake shrugged and took another sip of his wine. 'He can drop me off on the way. I only live in Mayfair.'

'I know,' Layla answered, her pretty mouth curving in yet another ironic little smile. 'I read it in the local newspaper. Lucky you.'

He hadn't mentioned that he lived in Mayfair to impress her, but he couldn't deny that he was peeved that she appeared so singularly *unimpressed*...dismissive, almost. It made him feel like the lead character in the

story *The Emperor's New Clothes*—a charlatan and a
liar hiding behind a façade of wealth and success. In
his mind he was still the poor boy living with a father
who beat him and despised him and locked him in his
bedroom in the dark when he wanted to exact particularly cruel punishment… His mouth tightened grimly
as he fought the tide of agonising memory that rolled
through him.

'If you find it so disagreeable to accept my offer of
a ride home in preference to catching a train then I'm
not going to argue with you. As soon as we've finished
eating I'll pay the bill and we can go. There's a tube
station just round the corner.'

When hot embarrassed colour visibly flooded into
her porcelain cheeks Drake firmly schooled himself not
to let it remotely disturb him…

CHAPTER FOUR

THEIR date had been an unmitigated disaster.

Layla wasn't quite sure what she had done to make Drake suddenly turn so cold towards her, but the fact was she'd definitely done something. He'd sat beside her in the car in chilling silence as his chauffeur dropped her off at the tube station. Even when she'd thanked him for the lovely meal and said goodbye he'd barely been able to bring himself to reciprocate. He'd merely murmured, 'Goodnight, Layla', and then glanced at her with those glacial grey eyes, as if wondering what on earth had possessed him to invite her out in the first place.

Now, hours after the date, she painfully tried to recall every word they'd spoken at dinner in a bid to discover where she had gone wrong. Several times she found herself revisiting Drake's comment that he lived in Mayfair, and eventually—regretfully—had to own that her tone might well have been a little mocking. In no way had he been showing off to her, yet Layla had responded to the comment as though he *had*.

Because of her sour experience in working for her previous boss, she subconsciously believed that *all* wealthy and powerful men were arrogant and conceited and should be brought down a peg or two. No wonder

Drake had decided to have nothing else to do with her. He probably thought she was an ignorant little fool. Though, to be fair, her remark had been an innocently thoughtless one, born out of her still feeling nervous and not just a little overwhelmed by him. No insult had been intended. But now she couldn't help but believe he would never contact her again.

'I'm taking an hour off at around eleven this morning for a meeting in my office. Can I leave you to hold the fort?'

Her brother's voice broke into her morose musing. As if waking from a deep trance, Layla blinked up at him. She'd been arranging some fresh muffins on a shelf in the glass cabinet on the counter when she'd started reflecting on her date with Drake and wondering if she should risk telephoning him to make an apology.

As Marc patiently waited for her to acknowledge his comment she dusted some icing sugar from her hands and forced a smile. 'Of course you can. We're fairly quiet this morning, as you can see.' She glanced across the café at the two middle-aged women seated on the comfy sofa—regulars of theirs, clearly enjoying their lattes and buttered currant buns and looking enviably content. Apart from them an elderly man and a teenage boy transfixed by his mobile phone were the only other customers.

'The meeting is with Drake Ashton. Did you remember that he was coming today? Only you've hardly said a word about your date last night.'

'Of course.' Layla's lips were suddenly numb. 'It's Thursday, isn't it?'

'Go to the top of the class!' Grinning, Marc wiped

the back of his hand across his brow. As usual his dark hair was slightly awry and uncombed, his black T-shirt crumpled and unironed.

'I ironed you a pile of clean T-shirts yesterday and left them on your bed,' she told him, her gaze raking his clothing. 'How come you're wearing that one? It looks like you slept in it. Don't you think you ought to change if you're having a meeting with Drake?'

'So it's *Drake* now, is it? Clearly you're on much more informal terms with him since your date, then? I had my doubts when I first saw you this morning— you looked like someone had died. That naturally led me to conclude that things hadn't gone well…which is why I haven't quizzed you about it.'

'Never mind about that.' Impatiently Layla glanced round at the clock on the wall behind her. 'He's going to be here in just under half an hour. You need to change out of that scruffy T-shirt and comb your hair and en-deavour to look a bit more presentable. That's if you want him to think you're serious about the business?'

'Of course I'm serious about it!' Marc scowled. 'Why do you think I don't sleep at night? Because I *like* going round looking like death warmed up?'

'I don't doubt your commitment. I know how much you care about making the café a success. I'm just say-ing that having the opportunity to talk to Drake Ashton is a chance that doesn't come along every day, so you need to make the most of it. Look…if you leave now you'll have just about enough time to change. Even if you don't feel confident, it'll help you feel miles better if you put on a clean and ironed shirt and comb your hair.'

'You're right.' Sighing, her brother planted a resounding kiss on her cheek. 'If Ashton arrives before I'm back, make him a nice cup of coffee and give him a bun, will you? Thanks, sis.'

As soon as Marc had left Layla checked her hair and eyeliner in her make-up mirror and tried hard to still the nerves that seized her at the knowledge that Drake was arriving in just a few short minutes for the promised meeting with her brother. *Would he even acknowledge her when he saw her?* she fretted. He'd been like the proverbial 'ice man' when he'd dropped her off at the tube station last night, and he hadn't made any attempt to ring her and clear the air.

Knowing she would be utterly miserable if she succumbed to her feelings of fear and doubt about how he might behave towards her, she swung round to the digital radio on the shelf behind her and turned it on. As a lively pop tune filled the air she determinedly busied herself making the area round the counter even more pristine and inviting than it was already.

Twenty minutes later, after another worrying lull in custom, the glass door at the entrance opened, bringing with it a strong blast of frosted air. A mellow September it was not. Already it felt more like the onset of winter. But right then Layla was hardly concerned about the unseasonal temperature. Not when the reason for the suddenly open door planted his tall, lithe physique in front of the counter and made her heart race with one of his compelling enigmatic smiles. Wearing a stylish chocolate-brown cashmere coat over a fine dark suit, the handsome architect looked good enough to eat. Her blood heated even before he opened his mouth to speak.

'Remember me?'

'Yes, I do. You're the man who cold-shouldered me at the end of our date last night.'

Even as the words left her lips Layla cursed herself for yet again blurting out the wrong thing. How could she have forgotten so soon that she'd intended to apologise for upsetting him—not greet him with a frosty accusation?

Drake's handsome brow creased a little, emphasising the two deep furrows there. 'I'm sorry about what happened…I really am. But I'm beginning to realize, Layla, that you have the propensity to rub me up the wrong way. Anyway, I should have called you straight afterwards and made amends. I wish I had. I certainly didn't want the evening to end the way it did.'

The regret in his voice was accompanied by a glance filled with such intense longing that Layla could hardly believe it was directed at her. It had the effect of making her limbs suddenly feel as though they'd been injected with a powerful muscle relaxant, and she put her hands out onto the counter to support herself.

'I sometimes don't think before I speak,' she murmured, reddening, 'and I wish I did. Whatever I said or did that upset you I'm genuinely sorry for it.'

He nodded. 'Then let's start again, shall we? I'm going to visit a couple of sites after I see your brother, and I'd like you to come with me. I think you'll be interested in hearing what's planned there. I'll drop you back here at the café afterwards. We'll be a couple of hours at most.'

'I'd love to come with you, but I can't take time off just like that.'

Glancing round at the two remaining customers in

the vicinity, Drake's grey eyes glinted with humour. 'Because you're madly busy? Don't worry—I'll clear it with your brother when I see him. Is he around?'

'He'll be here any minute now. He—he had to dash home for something. Can I get you a coffee while you're waiting for him?'

'That would be great. I'll have a strong Americano.'

'What about something to eat?'

The question seemed to put him in a trance. His hypnotised gaze suggested he'd suddenly been plunged into a compelling private world of his own—a dimension that utterly and completely absorbed him. The faraway look in his eyes inexplicably made Layla's heart ache. It was a bit like when his absorption in his technical drawings had put her in mind of a schoolboy concentrating hard on his homework.

She couldn't help frowning. 'Drake?'

'What?' Raking his fingers through his hair, he gave a rueful smile. 'I don't want any food, thanks. I've had some breakfast this morning. A coffee will be just fine.'

As if he was discomfited by his zoning out, he turned away, clearly intending to make for a nearby table. Layla stopped him in his tracks.

'Do you mind if I say something?'

Warily he turned back. 'Go ahead.'

'I'm not for one second telling you how to conduct your business, so please don't take this the wrong way, but Marc is a little fragile at the moment. He needs... well, he needs to hear something good...something that will help give him some hope for the café's future. I'm not asking you to completely sugar-coat your advice, because obviously he needs to hear the truth, but whatever you advise him…would you—could you please bear that in mind when you talk?'

Again he drove his fingers through his hair. Although his expression was thoughtful, he also seemed a little weary, she thought.

'There's no sugar-coating the pill in business, Layla,' he said, 'but whatever advice I give to your brother, you can rest assured it will be fair and considerate…helpful too I hope. Was that all?'

With a self-conscious nod she turned her attention back to the task of making his coffee…

It felt so good to have her near again. As he drove the Range-Rover through the winding roads skirting the town Drake stole several covetous glances at his passenger's arrestingly beautiful profile and now and then couldn't resist lowering his gaze to the long slender legs encased in snugly fitting black cord jeans. He breathed in her perfume. It could have been life-giving oxygen as far as he was concerned, and he felt almost high on it.

After countless hours of hardly being able to concentrate on anything at all but Layla—long hours made even worse by the sleepless night that inevitably followed such pointed introspection—he was walking on air because she'd agreed to accompany him today. It didn't matter that it was ostensibly for work, visiting the sites he'd been commissioned to rejuvenate with attractive affordable housing. How he hadn't caved in and rung her after they'd parted last night he didn't know. Except that he'd maybe had some idea of briefly punishing her with a show of indifference because he'd been so sure she'd been mocking him about living in

Mayfair. He'd convinced himself that her unimpressed attitude suggested that she knew exactly where he came from and wasn't going to let him forget it. But as soon as he'd set eyes on her again in the café, Drake had known it was *himself* that he'd punished. Now he was predisposed to be kinder.

'Warm enough?' he asked. The question earned him a sunny smile that was akin to the pleasure of eating hot buttered toast in front of a roaring fire—preferably with *her*.

'This car has a great heater. The car I share with my brother has a heater that wouldn't warm up a shoebox, let alone anything bigger. By the way, how did your meeting with him go?'

'It was fine.' Drake pursed his lips, amused. He might have known she wouldn't be able to resist asking him about it. 'I think I've given him some food for thought. It's now up to him whether he acts on what I suggested or not. Most of all, he's going to have to learn to be patient. Things take time to change for the better. By the way, we didn't just talk about the café. You came into the conversation a few times too, Layla. The way he lit up at just the mention of your name told me that he adores you.'

It was impossible to suppress the jealousy that churned in the pit of his stomach when he thought about Layla regarding her brother in the same heartfelt way. Never in his life had *he* been on the receiving end of such a devoted sentiment.

Her slim shoulders lifted in a shrug. 'I don't know if it's true that he adores me, but I admit that we've always been quite close. Do you have any brothers or sisters?'

'No.' Drake's hands automatically tightened on the steering wheel. 'I don't. I'm an only child, I'm afraid.'

'That doesn't have to be a negative. Perhaps your parents decided that they only wanted you? Or maybe the reason they only had you was because they couldn't have any more children?'

His companion's innocently voiced assumptions sent a cold, clammy shiver up his spine. 'I've no idea,' he answered tersely. *But he did.* Being intimately acquainted with his family's dysfunctional history, he knew only too well that neither of those scenarios was true. 'I never asked them.'

'And there's no possibility of you asking them now?'

'No. There isn't. My mother walked out years ago, when I was just six, and my dad died when I was a teenager.' It was hard to subdue the bitterness in his tone, and straight away he sensed the embarrassment and discomfort that his comments had inflicted on the woman sitting beside him.

'I'm sorry, Drake...'

The sigh she emitted sounded genuinely heartfelt.

'Forgive me for being so tactless. I had no idea about your background.'

'It all happened a long time ago now, and it's not exactly something I want to broadcast. I'd be grateful if you didn't share the information with anyone else. In any case, as you can see...' Turning his head briefly to observe her, he was instantly perturbed by the concern reflected back at him from her luminous brown eyes. 'I'm a big boy now, and I get on just fine without my parents being around.'

'You're a lot tougher than I am, then.' Her tone was

tinged with sadness and regret. 'I lost my mum when I was very young too. She contracted pneumonia after a bout of severe flu and never recovered. Then, when I was a teenager, I lost my dad. I still miss both of them more than I can say.'

Startled that her losses mirrored his own family scenario—albeit his mother hadn't died but simply walked out—Drake was torn between voicing the usual polite words of commiseration and pulling the car over and impelling Layla firmly into his arms. He was aching with an almost unholy need to do just that. The mere idea of having an opportunity to touch her soft skin and silky hair, to feel her mouth tremble beneath his with what he secretly hoped might be an inflammatory need similar to his own, was almost too powerful to ignore.

But, seeing they were nearing the site he'd proposed they visit together, all he did was say thoughtfully, 'I'm sorry you miss them so badly, but life goes on, doesn't it? We have to try and make the best of things. When bad things happen you can either wallow in the idea that you've been dealt a bad hand or you can be determined to rise above it. Personally speaking, I was never going to stay around here and regard myself as some kind of victim—no matter how difficult or challenging it was to rise above my circumstances.'

He drove into the large denuded area that had already been cleared in preparation for building and pulled up beside one of the several works vans belonging to the contractor he'd hired. A few feet away scaffolding waiting to be erected lay in precisely organised piles on the cold hard ground.

'We're here.' Silencing the engine, he turned to study

his passenger. 'I know the weather's not great, but I'd still like to show you the site and tell you what we've got planned. Are you still up for a look round with me?'

'Of course.' Peering out of the windscreen, she let a fond smile touch her lips. 'There used to be a great playground here when I was a kid. My brother and I sometimes walked all the way from our house to get to it. My dad was inevitably working, so during the school holidays after Mum was gone we were more or less left to our own devices. We used to think it was a bit of an adventure to go to the playground on our own, to tell you the truth. Do you remember it, Drake?'

'I do.'

His own memories of the playground that had once stood on the site were definitely not as fond as Layla's, he mused. He too had visited it on his own, but he hadn't made any friends when he was there. The other kids had probably been warned by their parents to stay away from the boy whose mother had left him and who had a father notorious for being bad-tempered and more often than not *drunk*.

Bringing his focus firmly back to the present, Drake returned his pretty companion's smile. 'By the way, you'll have to wear a hard hat…Health and Safety demands it, I'm afraid. I've got a spare in the boot.'

The word *cold* didn't come anywhere near to describing the effect of the slashing raw wind that cut into Layla's face as soon as she stepped out of the car onto the flattened muddied ground. Shivering hard, and reflecting on the vehemence in Drake's tone when he'd talked about rising above his circumstances after the devastating events of his childhood, she suddenly understood why his success must mean so much to him. From this rundown suburban no-man's land to Mayfair was no small achievement. In fact, thinking about the deprivation in the area—both socially and educationally—his accomplishment was nothing less than remarkable. Wrapping her arms round the insubstantial padded jacket she wore with her jeans, she shivered again, fervently wishing she'd had the foresight to wear something much warmer.

'Let's walk. Some exercise will help warm you up. Here, you'd better put this on first.'

As he came to stand in front of her she saw the glint of concern that mingled with wry amusement in his mercurial grey eyes and her blood started to pump hard even *before* she started to walk round the site. She was so disconcerted by the reaction that as she moved forward to take the spare headgear he was holding out she immediately tripped over a stone and almost fell. The only reason she didn't was because Drake's hands caught hold of her arms just in time to steady her. In the process he grabbed the hard hat she was carrying and threw it to the ground, along with his own, so that he could properly support her.

During those volatile few seconds time slowed to a terrifying immediacy that ripped away all possibility of thought. Instead Layla was aware only of the acutely erotic heat that poured into the air between them. It was a formidable force that was impossible to ignore.

When her shocked gaze fell onto Drake's, only to see the candid hunger that was laid bare in his eyes, she knew with a jolt that they were reflecting the same shocking, raw need that she was experiencing. His steel-like grip on her upper arms didn't lessen as his warm breath hit the icy air with visible little clouds of steam. She yearned to say something…*anything* to restore the situation to some semblance of recognisable normality before it was too late…before she succumbed to something she might live to regret. But the idea abruptly melted away when in that very same instant he took his hands away from her arms to cup them either side of her jaw. The surprising sensation of a couple of rough-edged calluses and warm smooth skin pressed against her cold face was a sensual revelation.

With a harsh breath that was a precursor to the inevitability of his next action, Drake crushed her mouth savagely beneath his.

The combined taste of his lips and tongue was immediately sexy and addictive. Like a heady smooth cognac that she couldn't stop herself craving even when she knew drinking it would likely get her into trouble.

Layla found herself in the midst of a sensually battering storm that threatened to rip her from her moorings for ever, and her ears were filled with the sound of her own breathless gasps as her hands curled possessively into Drake's cashmere coat in a desperate bid to bring his strong hard body even closer to hers. What she wouldn't give to be skin to skin with him right then, instead of wearing restrictive clothing that prevented them from touching each other as passionately as they craved. Even in the teeth of the cutting wind that blew around them the fire they'd lit between them surely blazed hot enough to keep even the most arctic temperatures at bay?

The clawing sexual need that suddenly consumed her rocked her with its force. With an indisputable sense of urgency Drake hurriedly unzipped her jacket and roughly palmed her breast. Even through her clothing his touch was like a lick of raw flame scorching her. With a rough groan he broke off the avaricious kiss that was threatening to get out of control. His mouth's desertion left Layla helplessly pining for more. But she didn't feel abandoned for long, because straight away he pushed her jacket collar aside and pressed his mouth to the juncture between her neck and shoulder.

His heat all but undid her there and then. At the same time as his lips moved seductively over that highly sensitive region he sank his teeth into her skin and bit her. If it hadn't been for the fact that both his hands were holding her fast by her hips she was sure she would have fainted from the sheer scorching pleasure of it. Yet a kernel of common sense somehow engineered its way into the dangerous fog of desire, and with her heart racing she freed herself from the circle of his arms and stepped away. As she moved back her hand gingerly touched the tender place where he'd bitten, feeling the sting that undoubtedly meant he'd left his mark. Her face flooded with violent heat.

'We shouldn't be doing this. We *can't* do this. You were—you were going to show me round the site and tell me about what's planned here. Perhaps we should concentrate on doing that instead of—instead of...'

'Wanting to rip each other's clothes off?'

Drake's throaty intonation and teasing smile came dangerously close to making Layla hungrily return to his arms. To prevent such an occurrence she made herself recall how devastated she'd been when her ex-boss had mercilessly persuaded her to invest her life savings in the financial scheme that had turned out to be totally crooked. The humiliating and hurtful memory reminded her of her vow to steer clear of wealthy charming men for as long as she lived. Better she fell for a factory worker or a postman so long as he was honest and true.

She'd already been burned by someone whose *raison d'être* was money and success, and she was in no hurry to experience a similar scenario.

'I don't know what came over me, but you can be sure it won't happen again. Shall we go and look round the site now? Time's getting on and I need to get back to work.'

She gave Drake the scantest glance she could manage, knowing that if she gazed too long into those magnetically compelling eyes of his her good intentions and warnings to herself would be crushed into oblivion and she would lose all ability to make sensible decisions where he was concerned for good.

'Come on, then.' He bent down to retrieve the hard hats he'd let fall to the ground. After placing one on his own head, he moved across to Layla and handed her hers. 'Put this on. We'll do what we came to do and walk round the site, then I'll take you back to the café. Later on tonight, when you've finished work, I'll ring you so we can talk about when to see each other again. And when we do, I'm going to absolutely insist that you let my driver collect you.'

'Didn't you hear what I said? What if I tell you I've decided I don't want to see you again?'

'I won't believe you. Not after what just happened between us.'

Drake's expression was as serious and formidable as she'd ever seen it. Layla's icily tipped fingers gripped the hard hat tightly, but she wouldn't put it on until she got her feelings off her chest.

'Let me put you straight about something. I'm not interested in having some meaningless sexual fling with you that will burn out in a few days or even a few weeks. I won't deny that I find you physically attractive, but that in itself isn't enough to persuade me that it's a good idea to see you again.'

'No? Then what is?'

'I'll only agree to see you if you let me into your life a little…if you give me the chance to get to know the man behind the successful veneer you present to the world. If you're willing to at least consider the possibility then I'll agree to another date with you. If not, then we may as well forget the whole thing.'

'Setting aside what I do for a living, and my public reputation, I'm a very private man, Layla. I very rarely let anyone get too close to me…especially women.'

He almost didn't need to say the words. Straight away she was aware of the turmoil that raged inside him at the mere notion of allowing her more intimate access into his life. It was as though she was the enemy and he was behind an impenetrable wall of steel keeping her from advancing any further.

Her breathing was suddenly uncomfortably shallow. 'So your previous relationships with women have been based on satisfying sexual desire and nothing more? Is that what you're telling me?'

'This really isn't the time or the place to discuss this.' Drake's troubled gaze turned into a warning glare. 'Right now I need to do my job and look round the site. I'll ring you later on tonight and we can talk then.'

Indignation that she was being palmed off until it was more convenient made Layla bristle. 'Don't bother. I'm not interested in being placated by your no doubt charmingly reasonable explanation as to why you don't want to let me get to know you properly, and neither am I interested in being some convenient bed partner while you're in town.' She unceremoniously shoved the hard hat into his hand. 'Don't worry about giving me a lift back to the café. The walk will do me good. I know the route back into town like the back of my hand.'

'Don't go.'

There was a heartfelt plea in his voice that stopped her in her tracks.

'Why? Why shouldn't I go?' she asked, her heart thudding inside her chest as though she teetered on the edge of a cliff.

'Because I want to show you round the site and explain what we've got planned to improve it.' He expelled a frustrated sigh. 'Aren't you at least interested in that?'

Even though she was mad at him, Layla couldn't deny that she was more than interested in the planned improvements. After all, she knew only too well what it would mean to the town and its downtrodden population. It would feel like a betrayal of everyone she knew who lived there to just walk away and pretend she didn't care.

Pushing her windblown hair out of her eyes, she

slowly nodded. 'Of course I'm interested. All right, then…I'll stay and let you show me around.'

Quirking a wary eyebrow, Drake smiled. 'And what about me ringing you later on tonight so we can talk about another date?'

'If you agree to seriously consider my request about letting me into your life a little…then, yes…you can ring me.'

Shaking his head, as if he knew it was pointless to pursue the matter further, Drake lightly placed his hand at Layla's back and led her onto the site.

CHAPTER FIVE

'So WHAT do you think of the planned improvements?' As he drove them out of the site, Drake stole an interested glance at his passenger and saw that her incandescent brown-eyed gaze was definitely reflective.

'I think it's terrific what you plan to do,' she replied enthusiastically. 'Especially the idea of having a communal garden with lots of lovely planting and an adjoining play area for the kids.'

'You don't think the kids will pull up the plants?'

'No, I don't. Give people a place to be proud to live in, a place that's aesthetically beautiful as well as practical, and in my view they'll do everything they can to take care of it. A lot of the smaller children I know love plants and flowers, and if someone shows them how to plant and water they'll love them even more.'

'So the plans have your personal seal of approval, Miss Jerome?'

Layla's pale cheeks were suddenly flooded with the most becoming shade of pink. 'You don't need my approval…but I'm glad you asked my opinion just the same.'

'There's one more place I'd like to show you before I take you back—a place that we're planning to improve as well. It's a short, nondescript side-street in one of the more rundown areas.'

'Okay.'

Drake's heart was thundering on the drive to the location where he'd been raised as a boy, but he tried to look beyond the now emptied shabby Victorian houses and envisage instead the more modern and attractive buildings he intended to erect in their place.

'This is the street you were talking about?' his companion asked, her expression puzzled as she peered through the windscreen.

'Yes. It's been empty for a long time now. Do you know someone who used to live here?' Immediately Drake prayed that she didn't. He didn't want her view of him tainted by some gossipmonger's lurid account of his family.

'I don't know anyone that lived here, but I know there are a few locals who are petitioning the council to save the buildings and have them renovated.'

His lips twisted ruefully. 'I heard about that. As well-meaning as those folks are, I'm afraid the petition has already been discarded.'

'Why?'

Taken aback by the look of horror on Layla's face, and a little rattled by it, Drake sighed. 'Because an independent party has purchased the entire street and has plans to demolish the houses and construct more contemporary residences in their place.'

'When did you hear that?' The huge brown eyes that had dazzled him right from the start widened in shocked disbelief.

'About three months ago…when I put in a bid to buy the street.'

Layla's even white teeth clamped down against the soft flesh of her plump lower lip and her slender hand pushed shakily through her hair. 'So *you're* the independent party?'

'Yes…I am.'

'And *you* plan to pull down these historic old buildings and replace them with cheap modern "Identi-Kit" houses with about as much character as cardboard eggboxes?'

Drake would have grinned in amusement if it weren't for the fact that Layla looked so painfully aggrieved. 'I hope I have a lot more taste than that,' he said dryly. 'And for your information I never build cheap modern houses…no matter where they're situated. First and foremost, it's important to me to build housing that residents will be proud to live in, and I always utilise the most skilled craftsmen I can find to build them— as well as using the very best materials.'

'Be that as it may, the Victorians knew how to build houses that stood the test of time and were elegant too, and I have to tell you that I'm one of the town's residents who petitioned the council. If you're planning on improving the area why can't you just invest your money in renovating what's already here?'

'Because I'd rather rebuild than renovate, that's why.'

'I don't understand. Why won't you consider renovating?'

Even though seeing Layla's obviously distressed glance was akin to being punched hard, and it had shocked him to learn that she had been one of the petitioners who had fought to keep the Victorian terraced houses rather than demolish them, Drake didn't feel up to explaining why he'd rather raze the old buildings to the ground and build new ones. He was feeling somewhat peeved that Layla should take it upon herself to advise him what to do. When he'd last looked, *he* was the architect in charge of helping to regenerate the town.

'I'd better get you back to the café,' he murmured.

'Why won't you answer my question? If you're planning on pulling down the houses you might at least have the courtesy to explain why.'

Turning to face her, Drake bit back his irritation as best as he could. 'I can see that you clearly have some romantic ideas about renovating these properties, but it takes a hell of a lot of money to restore old houses and bring them back to their former glory. Sometimes it's far more economical and easier to build new ones. Don't forget I'm a businessman as well as an architect, Layla.'

Before she had a chance to reply he gunned the engine and reversed the car rapidly down the street, and she glumly averted her gaze to stare out of the window…

Layla had asserted that she wanted him to let her into his life and to get to know the man behind the successful veneer. It was the single most scary thing that a woman had ever said to him.

Drake put down the tumbler with a double shot of whisky in it and morosely folded his arms.

Even scarier was the growing temptation to flirt with the idea of considering her request. But he was worried that after showing her the street where he'd grown up, and telling her he planned to demolish all the houses there and erect new ones, she'd change her mind about wanting to get to know him at all. She'd hardly taken the news of his plans for the street well. Yet it hadn't affected the powerful allure she still had for him. *Damn it all to hell!* Layla Jerome had put a spell on him…either that or he had somehow lost his mind.

The decision to return to the place of his birth to help regenerate the area was seriously backfiring on him. The *very* last thing he'd expected to happen was that he should end up seriously lusting after a beautiful local girl that worked in a café.

He'd come back to Mayfair after finishing work that evening, but he'd neither eaten nor showered. His mind, body and senses had been too caught up in a tornado of longing and lust to accomplish either of those fundamental things so he had headed out to a hotel bar he knew in a bid to hopefully distract himself. Eating held no appeal when there was so much churning going on in the pit of his stomach, and he hadn't showered because he didn't want to wash away the alluring scent of Layla's body. Her seductive smell was all over him, and if he shut his eyes he could recall the wonderful sensation of her soft velvety skin beneath his fingertips and the incredible taste of her sexy mouth…

A bolt of inflammatory need shot straight to his loins and Drake silently cursed the ill-timed inconvenience of it. Even though she'd firmly told him that she wasn't interested in a sexual fling that would last only a few days or weeks he was still hoping to get her into bed soon. She'd asserted that she wanted to get to know him, but he knew if he let her she would probably be extremely uneasy with the taciturn, insecure man behind the glamorous and successful reputation—a man who was still too haunted by his past to be anywhere near comfortable with the idea of making a serious commitment to a woman.

Glancing impatiently down at his watch, and seeing that it was much later than he'd thought, he lifted the glass he'd put beside him on the bar and drank down the remaining contents in one hit. Even though Layla had been less than warm towards him when he'd dropped her off at the café, Drake had insisted he would ring her, and if he left it any later he knew he probably wouldn't get to speak to her at all tonight.

'Had a bad day?'

He glanced round in surprise at the shapely blonde who lowered herself onto the barstool next to him. She wore a fitted silver-grey suit over a dark red shirt with a revealing neckline, displaying enough décolletage to start a small stampede. *Except that the provocative sight left Drake completely cold.* There was only one woman he would head up a small stampede for and that was Layla.

'It wasn't all bad,' he drawled laconically, getting to his feet, 'there were definitely some highlights.'

'You're not leaving?'

The pneumatic blonde didn't try to hide her disappointment. But once on his feet Drake knew emphatically what was next on his personal agenda—and it wasn't whiling away the evening in a bar making small talk with a woman who was clearly on the lookout for a profitable sexual encounter with someone.

'I'm afraid I am. Have a nice evening,' he murmured,

the automatic half-smile that touched his lips quickly fading because all he could think about was getting back home and phoning Layla.

'She's gone to bed?'

On receiving this astounding information from Layla's brother Marc, Drake stopped stirring the mug of strong black coffee he'd made and turned round to lean back against the marble-topped counter in the kitchen.

Feeling stunned and aggrieved at the same time, he couldn't help the irritation that seeped into his reply. 'What do you mean, she's gone to bed? It's barely after ten.'

'She's never been able to hack staying up late. She's a real morning person.'

'And how is it that you're answering her mobile? Is she staying with you at the moment?'

'We share a house. I have the ground floor and Layla the top. Didn't she tell you that?'

'No. She didn't. Anyway, morning person or not, I'd appreciate it if you'd go upstairs and see if she's still awake. I told her to expect my call,' he said, mustering as much authority as he was able—because he was still reeling at the notion of her going to bed and apparently not being the slightest bit perturbed that he hadn't rung earlier. Was it because she was still mad at him for wanting to knock the terraced houses down and build new ones?

'I can't do that, I'm afraid. I've got strict instructions not to. That's why she left her phone with me. She said if you rang I was to tell you that she'll ring you on Monday. I'm really sorry, Mr Ashton, but it's more than my life's worth to disturb her. You may not know this yet, but my sister's got a real temper on her. Trust me—glass can be shattered when she loses it!'

Drake clenched his jaw and curled his palm into an angry fist down by his side. She was going to ring him on *Monday*? Was she playing some kind of game with him that entailed teaching him a lesson for not agreeing to renovate the Victorian terraced houses? he wondered. Could she even *guess* at the depth of frustration she'd left him with earlier today? More to the point, did she believe that her request that he let her get to know him had frightened him off? Clearly if it *had* she certainly wasn't going to lose any sleep over it.

'Okay. Thanks,' he muttered, finding himself completely at a loss to know what else to say.

Crossly replacing the receiver, he dropped down into a nearby chair. *Did she really mean to let an entire weekend go by before she saw him again?* He scowled. If he'd had her address and had been anywhere near the vicinity of her home he would have considered battering down her door to *make* her come and speak to him if he had to…*temper* or no. He wasn't about to let a potential display of volatile emotion put him off his goal. Besides which, the mere idea of Layla losing her temper instigated an immediate fantasy of him subduing it with a long, lazy open-mouthed kiss on that sexy mouth of hers.

Having already sampled her exquisite taste, the fantasy was almost too real to be borne. Releasing a hard to contain groan, Drake pushed impatiently to his feet.

The hot leisurely shower he'd envisaged was going to have to be replaced by one closer to sub-zero temperatures if his frustration was going to be remotely eased tonight...

Layla released a long sigh of relief when Marc told her the next morning that Drake had rung. She'd gone to bed early because she'd been genuinely tired, but she'd also been irritated with him because he wouldn't consider renovating the Victorian terrace. It was clear he was also aggravated with her, because she'd asserted that she wanted to get to know him, that she wasn't just interested in a short-term fling.

The man clearly had issues around allowing a woman to get too close to him and Layla wanted to find out *why*. She also wanted to know why he wouldn't consider renovating the Victorian terrace. Somehow she didn't buy it that it was more profitable to build new residences in its place. Drake might be a businessman as well as an architect, but she didn't believe that financial consideration was the *only* reason he wouldn't look at renovation.

Still, at the end of the day the man was doing far more for the town than anyone had in too many years to mention, and even if she was upset he wouldn't listen to a small local petition to keep the terraced houses she couldn't let that taint her feelings towards him... not when she sensed deep down that he was a genuinely good man.

It was while she was clearing away the debris of her breakfast and stacking the dishwasher that a sudden idea took hold. Maybe it was time she played a more proactive part in their association? Perhaps it was time to turn the tables and this time surprise *him*? She decided that if anything at all was going to come from their association—be it an irresistible and unforgettable fling or a mutual commitment to a much more meaningful relationship—she wanted at least to have joint command of it. Never again would she allow a man's desires to take precedence over her own wants and needs—or, as in the case of her unscrupulous ex-boss, to convince her that *he* knew best.

In particularly good spirits that day, Marc agreed to let her have the afternoon off. He even gave her an affectionate hug when she confessed she was going up to London to see Drake.

'I like him. He's a very astute businessman,' he said, smiling. 'He told me I shouldn't be in a hurry to throw in the towel and sell the café just because the takings are down. At any rate it isn't a good time to sell, and I'd only get peanuts for it. He explained that the whole point of regenerating the area was not just to encourage new residents to move here, but to encourage more successful and appealing retail outlets to inhabit the high street and sell their goods. The influx of new customers would help small businesses like the café become more thriving concerns. "Give it a couple of years at least to see if things work out," he advised. So that's what I'm going to do. I can't tell you how much better I feel at having some direction at last. Say thanks again for me when you see him, won't you?'

The fact that Marc was more than happy at the advice Drake had given him went a long way to firming

Layla's decision to pay him an impromptu visit. In any case, after that smouldering encounter with him yesterday at the building site she knew it was pointless to pretend she wasn't aching to see him again. And she'd dearly love to find out a bit more about his background and childhood if she could. Sometimes he had a near haunted expression in his eyes—a faraway look that suggested he was tormented by some unspoken grief. Did his painful reflections dwell on memories of a troubled past? she wondered.

When the taxi dropped her off outside the stunning hexagonal building Drake had designed, she almost wished she had a stiff drink at hand to give her some Dutch courage. What if he didn't welcome this spontaneous visit of hers and was mad at her for turning up unannounced? Should she at least have rung him to let him know she was coming? *Then it wouldn't have been a surprise.*

Layla softly murmured that thought out loud.

A few minutes later, travelling in the swish modern lift up to Drake's floor, she stole a glance in the mirrored interior to check her appearance. She'd left her shoulder-length dark hair loose today, and it helped cover the small pink abrasion that Drake had so passionately gifted her with. Carefully pushing aside some silken strands, she let her fingers tenderly examine it. Then, feeling somehow guilty, she let her hair fall back into place to hide it.

In a bid to appear a little more relaxed than she had been when Drake had taken her out to dinner, she'd opted to wear light blue denims and a plain white shirt with a lined fawn-coloured trench-coat for her spontaneous visit. But when her gaze honed in on the softly scarlet bloom that highlighted her cheeks, she stopped focusing on her appearance and looked away with a frown.

It had been her hope to present an image of relaxed composure when she saw him, but now there was no chance of that. Why, oh, why could she never seem to prevent her feelings from showing on her face like some people could? Forget composure. Her big-eyed 'caught in the headlamps' expression made her resemble a frightened rabbit rather than a determined young woman intent on taking a potentially volatile situation firmly into her own hands…

'Do you have an appointment with Mr Ashton?'

Drake's efficient, intimidating blonde secretary was like a sentry at the gates of Rome, suddenly alerted to an impending invasion. As she stood behind the desk with her arms folded her diamond chip blue eyes sternly raked over Layla's appearance, as if silently warning her that it was going to take a minor miracle to get past *her* to see Drake.

'No, I don't.' Swallowing hard, Layla knew her smile was uncertain and strained. 'I thought—I thought I'd surprise him.'

The sound of Drake's deep voice suddenly bellowing at someone behind the closed glass door that she knew led into his office made her start. The secretary's coral painted lips stretched briefly in an ironic smile.

'Somehow I don't think my boss is remotely in the mood for surprises, Miss…?'

'Jerome.'

'Yes, of course. You were here the other evening, weren't you? Except he *was* expecting you then.'

'Yes. He was. Look, I've come a long way to see him today. Can you at least tell him that I'm here?'

'I know you must be a friend of his, but I'm afraid I can't. His diary is full for the whole afternoon. Why don't you leave your phone number? Or you can write a message if you'd prefer? I'll make sure that he gets it.'

The other woman perfunctorily pushed a lined pad and a pen across the contemporary glass desk that right then seemed to symbolise an insurmountable barrier Layla couldn't cross. Frozen by indecision, her teeth worrying at her lip, she numbly picked up the pen, then stared down at the writing paper feeling wretched. It had obviously not been one of her better decisions to turn up at Drake's office unannounced. Perhaps she could find a café somewhere nearby and try to reach him on his mobile?

Just as she leant over the pad to write a message his office door opened and he stepped out. Wearing a sky-blue fitted sweater that hugged his hard-muscled lean frame, and dark blue jeans that highlighted his strong long-boned thighs, he too was dressed much more informally today. But she barely had time to realise much else, because he came to an immediate standstill and stared at her as if he couldn't believe his eyes. His piercing silvery gaze made her insides flutter wildly. Behind him, a well-built man dressed in a grey pinstriped suit, carrying what looked like some rolled-up technical drawings, stole the chance to slip away discreetly before his boss noticed that he was gone.

'Layla. To what do I owe the honour?' Drake's almost languorous drawl was tinged with the faintest mockery.

Lying the pen back down on the pad, Layla quelled the flurry of nerves that seized her and straightened up to face him. 'I thought I'd surprise you,' she told him.

'Well, you've certainly accomplished that.'

'I missed your call last night.'

'Yes, you did. Still…you're here now. Do you want some coffee?'

Before Layla had the chance to reply he turned to his secretary and said, 'Monica? Can you get me and my visitor some coffee, please?'

'Have you forgotten that you've got an appointment with Sir Edwin Dodd in twenty minutes, Mr Ashton?'

'Ring him and put him off, will you? Tell him something important has come up.'

The efficient Monica couldn't hide her dismay, or the fact that she was suddenly quite flustered. Layla almost felt sorry for her.

'This is a longstanding appointment…don't you remember? He's probably already on his way, and I don't think he'll take too kindly to being put off at the last minute.'

As he folded his arms her boss's glance was formidably steely. 'Am I labouring under the misconception that *I'm* the one in charge round here?'

'Of course not. I apologise if I was a little too blunt. I'll ring Sir Edwin straight away and make your apologies. Then I'll get your coffee.'

'Thank you.' He directed his gaze back to Layla, and the faintest enigmatic smile touched Drake's lips. 'Why don't you come into my office?'

Following her into the stunning room, with its pan-
oramic view of rooftops and a gloriously cloudless blue
sky, he quietly shut the door behind them. 'It's good to
see you—if a little unexpected. Let me take your coat
and bag.'

As soon as Layla had unbuttoned the fawn trench-
coat she sensed Drake move behind her to help remove
it from her shoulders. The potent mix of warm virile
man, sexy cologne and the electrifying brush of his
hands through the layers of her clothing made her feel
quite faint with desire. It was extremely difficult to
think straight above such a shockingly imperative need.

In contrast, Drake appeared almost to want to taunt
her by moving deliberately slowly, his air definitely
preoccupied. But after carefully folding her coat over
the arm of a nearby chair, and depositing her shoulder-
bag and tote on the seat, he finally returned to stand in
front of her. Dropping his hands to his lean masculine
hips, he released a long drawn-out sigh. 'Well, well,
well… You certainly know how to keep me on my toes,
Layla Jerome.'

Fiddling with the ends of her hair, she couldn't prevent the heat that flooded into her face. 'I'm sorry. I
should have rung you first.'

'Then your appearance would hardly have been a
surprise, would it?'

'No, it wouldn't.'

'Besides…I definitely get the impression that talking on the phone isn't exactly a favourite occupation
of yours.'

Moving nearer, Drake curled his hands round her

slim upper arms and slowly but firmly brought her body in closer to his. Layla caught her breath.

'I wanted to wring your brother's neck when he wouldn't go and tell you that I wanted to talk to you,' he confessed huskily.

'It wasn't his fault. I told him not to disturb me.'

'And why did you do that, I wonder? Was it because you were angry that I was going to have those houses demolished in preference to renovating them?'

'I don't deny I was furious about that. I know you left our forgotten little town a long time ago, but there are a lot of things that I still love about it. One of them is the rundown shabby streets with their once beautiful and historic old houses. It makes me terribly sad to think about the hardworking families who once lived in them and experienced all their joys and sorrows there but are now all gone.'

'Do you know for a fact that they were *all* hardworking and happy?' Drake asked, gravel-voiced.

There was something in his tone that made Layla's stomach drop. 'No, I don't. I just—'

'I grew up in that shabby little street, in one of those once "beautiful and historic old houses". As I recall, it wasn't remotely beautiful when I lived in it. Unfortunately I didn't experience much joy there either…plenty of sorrow, yes. And my father *definitely* wasn't hardworking.'

'I'm sorry to hear that. I didn't mean to rub salt into any wounds by expressing my opinions, Drake.'

'Forget about it. Like you said, the ghosts of the past are all gone now. So, tell me, do you usually go to bed so early?'

The humour that replaced the pain in his eyes lifted her heart after the sad confession about his home-life. At least she now knew why he was so determined to demolish those houses.

'During the week when I work I always go to bed early. I know you wanted to speak to me last night, but do you really think talking on the phone is the best way to get to know someone? I personally prefer to talk to my friends face to face...especially when it comes to discussing something personal.'

Drake's answering short laugh made all the hairs stand up on the back of her neck.

'So it's my *friend* you want to be now, is it?'

Brushing her hair out of the way, he laid his hand over her cheek, gently stroking the pad of his thumb down over her flushed skin, eliciting an explosion of goosebumps.

'I'll only agree to be your *friend*, Layla, if I'm afforded certain...shall we say...privileges?' he said, smiling.

As enticing as the idea to afford him those privileges was, Layla determinedly held her ground, even though his touch was seriously making her melt. 'I think that comment sounds very much like an avoidance strategy to me.'

'You think I'm avoiding something, do you? What am I avoiding?' With an incorrigible grin he moved his hand to rest it lightly on her shoulder.

'Answering the question I asked you yesterday—about—about letting me get to know you...giving me the chance to see the real man behind the successful architect.'

Once again she caught her breath as she waited for his reply. His grin faded almost immediately and his grey eyes suddenly acquired a glint of terrifying sadness that made her stomach roll over.

'That question ensured I barely slept a wink last night,' he told her gruffly.

'Why?' she whispered.

'Before I answer that, I have a question for you… Why did you give up a presumably well-paid job in London to move back home? What happened with this boss of yours? You said he wasn't a boyfriend, but I get the feeling something intimate happened between you. Was it an affair that perhaps turned sour?'

Drake's hands were suddenly fastening round her arms again, and his grip noticeably tightened, making her heart thump. 'I didn't have an affair with him. I just—he plied me with drink at an office party and I stupidly succumbed to sleeping with him. It was only the one time, and I hated myself for it straight after.'

Feeling angry that Drake had turned the tables on her, Layla tried to twist free, but he was having none of it and held her fast.

'My boss was like a lot of men who have wealth and power. He thought it was a golden ticket to having anything he wanted, and no doubt after my refusing his requests for a date for so long it helped boost his ego to get me drunk and finally persuade me into his bed.' Her face was suffused with embarrassed heat. 'I despise myself for being so weak, because he was the most unscrupulous and unprincipled man I've ever met.'

'Was that the reason you quit your job?'

Sucking in a steadying breath as the memory of the

shameful betrayal that had finally forced her to leave washed over her, she gazed into Drake's eyes with an unwavering furious stare.

'No. At least, it wasn't the main one. In another stupidly weak moment I let him persuade me to invest all my savings in a deal that was a total scam from start to finish. When I lost every penny, he shrugged as if he couldn't care less and said, "That's the business we're in, Layla. It's all about risk. Sometimes we win and sometimes we lose. You should have known that…silly girl." He wasn't wrong there.' She shook her head bitterly. 'I *was* silly… Let me rephrase that. I was utterly and unforgivably stupid. My common sense deserted me. But at the time I invested in his deal I'd long grown tired of the soulless nature of my job *and* my boss. I was desperate to leave. I wanted to retrain as a youth worker or something along those lines instead…something that could be of use to people. But I knew if I was going to study I'd need money to support myself. That's why I fell for my boss's expert sales pitch. I thought that because he'd reached the heights as a broker, and made a lot of money by speculating and taking risks himself, he must know what he was doing. I never thought for one minute that he might take me to the cleaners because I only slept with him once and refused to do so again. It's amazing what we can convince ourselves of when we're desperate, isn't it?'

'I'm sorry.'

The comment sounded genuinely compassionate, and Drake's firm grip on her arms gentled.

'Not half as sorry as I am. I know one thing for sure. I'll never make a decision out of desperation again.'

'You did nothing wrong, Layla. It's your low-life ex-boss that needs hanging out to dry.'

'Anyway...' She lifted a shoulder in a shrug. 'You live and learn, as my dad always used to say. Are you going to answer *my* question now, Drake?'

Withdrawing his hands, he pressed his fingers deep against his temples. For the first time since he'd appeared in the outer office she noticed the softly bruised shadows beneath his eyes that denoted his previous night's lack of sleep.

'I've been giving it some serious thought.'

Not brave enough to prompt him, Layla neither moved nor spoke.

Lifting his strong cut-glass jaw, Drake gave her one of his searing, compelling glances. 'I want you Layla. I'm sure you know that only too well by now. You're like a fever in my blood that I can't recover from. So I've decided that I will give you more access than I've given to any other woman before and let you get to know me a little. But I want to make it clear that that *doesn't* mean there'll be no holds barred—because it's quite likely there will be.' The glitter in his eyes that followed this statement was almost fierce. 'I don't share my feelings or my thoughts easily. Maybe that's a habit I'll eventually learn to break, but there'll definitely be boundaries if we become more intimate. Think you can handle that?'

With her heart bumping heavily against her ribs, Layla found herself nodding slowly. 'Yes, I do. At least, I'm willing to take the risk.'

CHAPTER SIX

AFTER they had their coffee Drake gave Layla the 'grand tour' of his offices, because he knew if they stayed alone together any longer, cloistered in his private domain, he wouldn't be able to keep his hands off her. As it was he had to contend with the too interested glances of his colleagues...*especially* the men. But how could he blame them when her slim-hipped jeans-clad figure and beautiful face was a magnet for any male with a pulse? No matter how young or old...

From the moment he'd told her that he was willing to let her get to know him—barring one or two no-go areas that he hadn't yet outlined—he'd begun to feel uncharacteristically possessive towards her. It was a new sensation for Drake, and one he'd never experienced before—not even with his ex Kirsty.

As they toured the offices on each floor Layla appeared genuinely fascinated by the different projects his architects and designers were undertaking—taking him and them aback by asking the kind of in-depth questions that he asked his clients himself in a bid to ascertain their construction needs. She was particularly interested in the social and environmental aspects of the various designs, and his younger male architects were only too happy to oblige her with full-length explanations, he saw. The realisation made him proud that he'd hired such good people, but it also made him intensely jealous that they were practically falling over themselves to interact with Layla.

When she stood beside them to examine an architectural model more closely, or leant over their shoulders to view a design or a technical drawing on a computer, did their hearts pound because she was so near as his always did?

He couldn't wait to have her to himself again, and after a couple of hours of this self-inflicted torture Drake was more than ready for them to return to his office.

By the time they reached the executive floor he noted that it was nearing six in the evening and one or two people were packing up for the day, ready to go home. Monica looked decidedly disgruntled as he and Layla arrived back in the outer office, giving him the instant vibe that she wasn't too impressed with his impromptu tour.

'I've rescheduled Sir Edwin Dodd for Monday afternoon at two, but the other appointments you so unfortunately missed all ask if you could call them personally to establish when you'll definitely be available. Other than that…*All Quiet on the Western Front*, as they say— and unless there's anything urgent I'm going home.'

'Thank you, Monica,' he replied, smiling. 'I appreciate your hard work today. I know it can't have been easy cancelling my appointments at the last minute. Are those the phone numbers of the clients that I missed?'

He gestured towards the piece of paper she was holding out to him.

'Yes.' She perfunctorily handed it over, then impatiently hovered as he scanned down the printed list.

'That's fine. Thanks again,' he murmured.

'I'll say goodnight, then.'

Without further ado she slipped on her raincoat, arranged the strap of her bag securely over her shoulder, then exited the office without so much as a backward glance at either him or Layla.

Striding back into his private office, Drake dropped the paper onto his desk and then called out to his guest to come and join him.

'I get the feeling that your secretary's going to view me as enemy number one should I ever dare visit you here again…especially without an appointment.' Stepping into the room and then quietly closing the door behind her, Layla shaped her mouth into a lopsided and rueful smile.

'She runs a tight ship.' Drake grinned. 'She doesn't like it when her captain goes AWOL.'

'I can't say I blame her. You probably missed several important appointments today.'

'Do you really think I care about that right now?'

Planting himself directly in front of her, Drake could no longer resist the impulse to be closer. Watching her talking and smiling with his colleagues had been excruciating torment because he hadn't been free to touch and hold her as he yearned to do. He hadn't even dared catch her eye in case he revealed his longing in front of the people he was ultra-careful to keep his private life a firmly closed book to. At any rate, he fully intended to make up for that self-denial now.

He started by cupping Layla's small, delicately made jaw, and straight away saw her eyes darken and grow even more lustrous beneath the long ebony lashes that swept down over them. His pulse quickened. The sensual silken texture of her skin beneath his fingers made him long to explore all of her without restraint, to drown in her beauty and get drunk on it without the fear of consequences to either his heart or his conscience.

'You mesmerised them out there,' he told her. 'You're going to be the talk of the place for weeks to come.'

'I hardly think so.'

'Then you clearly don't know a lot about the male of the species.'

'That's probably true.'

Her dark eyes were troubled for a moment, and Drake could have kicked himself for reminding her of her dishonest ex-boss.

'Returning to the present, I hope you haven't made any plans for the weekend?' he commented, lowering his voice, holding her gaze with invisible ties that hungrily bound it to his.

'Why's that?'

'Because I'd like you to spend it with me.'

'All of it?'

The wonderment in her voice made Drake chuckle. 'Yes, all of it. And I'll make sure you get home early enough on Sunday that you can get to bed at your usual time.'

'So you're expecting me to stay the night with you? I mean…not just one night but two?'

'Think you could bear it?' He hated the doubt that suddenly surfaced in his mind. He wished he could shoot it dead. 'My house has several guest rooms. If you'd rather we didn't share a room until you get to know me better, then I want you to know I'll respect that.'

'Thanks.'

The gratefully innocent smile she gave him told Drake that he'd said the right thing. He was immensely relieved. He didn't want any more of their days or their evenings together to end in quarrels or disappointment. He'd rather suffer the torment of frustration than that.

'Do I get a kiss for being so thoughtful and considerate?' he teased, smiling.

In answer, Layla reached up on tiptoe and pressed her lips softly against his. Even though his first impulse was to ravish and plunder now that she'd agreed to his request, he summoned some stoic restraint from God only knew where and deliberately kept the kiss on the right side of slow and tender. But even so his hands moved up and down her back, and now and then ventured over the enticing curve of her delectable derrière.

'Time's getting on,' she murmured. 'Shouldn't we go and get something to eat?'

Reluctantly freeing her lips from the sensuous, erotic glide of Drake's gentle and surprisingly tender response to her kiss, Layla found herself staring up at him, noting the tiny bead of sweat glistening in the indentation above his carved top lip and the beginnings of five o'clock shadow already darkening his firm lower jaw. But most of all she registered the carnal hunger his mercurial grey eyes radiated back at her, and wondered how he'd managed to keep it at bay and kiss her with such tender restraint. If the tenor of that lovely kiss had been transformed at any point into a conflagration such as they'd ignited at the building site yesterday, she didn't doubt that her suggestion of getting something to eat wouldn't have been the very first suggestion she made...

Although genuinely relieved when Drake had stipulated he didn't expect them to share a room and that she might like to get to know him a bit better before they became more intimate, she was still breathless at his invitation to stay the night. Not just one night, but two. Funny how things worked out, she mused. When she'd been readying herself to travel up to London to pay him a spontaneous visit she'd somehow found herself packing a toothbrush and a spare pair of undies into her tote...*just in case.* She hadn't been behaving presumptuously, she told herself, just being sensibly prepared for an eventuality such as this. It was surely the practical thing to do when all Layla had to do was glance at the man for her to crave the most lascivious attentions imaginable.

Already it seemed that her vow to be cautious and utilise her common sense around him was seriously coming under fire.

'That sounds like a good idea. How about we go back to my place and I'll cook us something?'

'You can cook?'

His eyes flashed with humour. 'Don't get your hopes up. I'm a million light years away from Cordon Bleu, but I can do basic stuff like a stir fry and spaghetti bolognaise. And if you've got a sweet tooth I have some artisan vanilla ice cream in the fridge.'

'Then lead the way, Chef. My palate is all yours!'

Giving him a teasing grin, Layla moved across to the chair where Drake had left her black leather tote. But before she lifted it, Drake stepped up behind her and reached for her coat.

'Let me help you put this on.'

'Thanks.' She breathed in the heat from his body, along with his arresting cologne, and briefly shut her eyes tight to savour the moment.

'Let's go.' Catching her by her shoulders to spin her round, he dropped a light kiss onto her forehead and smiled.

It was dusk by the time Drake's chauffeur Jimmy pulled up outside the house. Stepping out onto the pavement, Layla registered that the air was surprisingly warm as opposed to the wintry feel of yesterday, when she'd visited the building site with Drake. Her heart leapt with pleasure, because it seemed like a good omen, but her attention was quickly diverted from the balmy temperature to the arresting sight of the impressive Georgian house that loomed up before her.

It was positioned at the end of a precisely mown lawn, with an ornate stone fountain at its centre. The building itself was a perfectly proportioned five-storeyed, elegant townhouse, with large picture windows and a subtly painted green front door that had a carved sunburst pediment above it. The Regency terrace where it was situated was surely one of the best addresses in London, she mused.

Sensing Drake come to stand silently beside her, Layla made sure her tone was perfectly innocuous when she said, 'So this is where you live? It's beautiful.'

'Why don't you come in and see if the inside matches that impression?'

Before she even stepped through the door Layla knew that it would. But what she hadn't expected was that the interior of such a traditional house would be decorated with such an eclectic mix of both traditional *and* modern furnishings and fittings. This was evidenced by the extremely contemporary black metal coatstand that might have been a sculpture standing just inside the door and the beautiful rosewood Regency armchair—both resting against a white marble floor that wouldn't have looked out of place in a luxurious Italian villa.

As Drake led her down the hall to the foot of a staircase with a tasteful green and gold runner, she saw to her surprise that instead of a balustrade it had a sheer glass wall running alongside it. She couldn't help turning towards her companion with a quizzical smile. 'You're a conundrum—you know that?'

His brow furrowed. 'What do you mean?'

'Well...' Sighing thoughtfully, she deliberately chose her words with care. No way did she want to make another inadvertent blunder and offend him. 'You design these incredible state-of-the-art modern buildings, yet you live in a very traditional nineteenth-century house. And when you walk through the door there's another surprise. Instead of traditional furnishings you've plumped for a real mix of old and new. It intrigues me. *You* intrigue me.'

Reaching towards her, Drake all but stopped her breath when he slowly and deliberately tucked some dark strands of her silky hair behind her ear. His silvery eyes glinted with warmth and humour, but Layla detected a surprising hint of vulnerability in the fascinating depths too—a vulnerability that he had to take great pains to keep hidden from the world at large, she was sure.

'I'm very glad that I intrigue you,' he replied. 'Whilst I don't see my wealth and position as some kind of "golden ticket" to get me anything I want, as your ex-boss did, I'll happily accept any advantages that might act in my favour. At least where you're concerned, Layla.'

When he said such seductive things to her he made it very hard for her to gather her thoughts. 'So why do you live in a house like this when you're renowned for designing some of the most contemporary buildings on the planet? That's what I'd like to know.'

'The watchwords for the Regency era were proportion, symmetry and harmony. I rather like that. As well as the desire for aesthetic beauty that the architects used as their guide, there's something very comforting and solid about the houses that were constructed then. But I also like the challenge of modernity…designing buildings that meet more contemporary needs—such as larger spaces to live and work in with plenty of light.' Drake's well-shaped mouth shaped a grin. 'But that's enough talk about design for one day. It feels too much like work. I don't know about you, but my stomach is crying out for some food. Let me show you round the rest of the house, then I'll go and cook our dinner.'

'I admit I'd love something to eat—but I'd also love to see what else you've done here.'

'Then I'll lead the way. But first give me your coat. You can leave your bag on the chair there.' Waiting until Layla had done just that, Drake gestured her to ascend the staircase in front of him. 'It will be my pleasure to show you round.'

After showing Layla three bathrooms with freestanding baths and every conceivable modern convenience that anyone could wish for, several bedrooms with chic French-style beds and original oil paintings on the walls, then a frighteningly elegant living room with exposed brick and French doors that led out onto a charming decked terrace, Drake proposed that they see the rest of the house after they'd eaten. So with that in mind they headed for the kitchen, where he proceeded to extract the ingredients for the stir-fry they'd agreed on from a large stainless steel refrigerator.

The kitchen was another testament to Layla's host's eclectic good taste. Every cabinet, piece of furniture and furnishing had clearly been positioned and designed to complement each other—from the glossed white and grey surfaces of the worktops to the arctic-white marble floor. But in contrast to the highly contemporary look that was one's first impression on entering the room, the evidence of several small antique oils of horses in the park here and there, and a typically high Regency ceiling that hinted at a much more gracious era, reminded visitors that they were in the home of a man who was not wholly mesmerised by designs from the twenty-first century alone.

'I love your home, Drake. I think it's the most interesting house I've ever been in,' Layla declared as she
watched him reach up to a cabinet for a large stainless
steel wok.

Setting the pan down on top of an unlit burner, he
turned to face her. 'Can I ask what you mean by "interesting"?'

His furrowed brow wore a frown, and she had the
distinct feeling that her comment had perturbed him in
some way. 'I just mean that it's not the kind of house
I expected you to live in, but I really like it...*and* how
you've decorated it. That's all.'

'You don't think there's something missing?'

'Like what?'

Dropping his hands to his hips, Drake studied her
intently. 'I don't know...warmth, perhaps? Some personal attribute that makes it feel more like a home?'

Intuiting what he was getting at, Layla felt her heart
immediately go out to him. 'Do you believe that you
lack warmth, Drake?' she asked softly.

Clearing his throat, he tunnelled his fingers restlessly through his hair. 'I've lived alone for so long.
Sometimes it concerns me that I've become a little too
insular. How can I be the best architect I can be if I lose
touch with what people really want in a home?'

The statement stunned her. 'You *are* the best architect. Surely your considerable catalogue of work must
tell you that? Isn't that why you were commissioned to
help regenerate our town?'

The tentative half-smile he gave her was definitely
uneasy. 'I don't know why I said what I did. Put it down
to me being at work since six this morning. I'm not com-

plaining, but it's been a hell of a long day. Anyway, I ought to crack on with cooking our meal.'

'Is warmth what *you* want in a home?' Layla ventured, her heart bumping beneath her ribs. 'Is it something that you maybe didn't experience as a child?'

The answering warning flash in his eyes was instant and intimidating—like burning embers from a fire that could potentially be dangerous to anyone sitting too close to the flames.

'Remember I told you there were areas in my life where you absolutely don't go? I'm afraid that's one of them.'

Giving his comment her utmost consideration, Layla frowned. 'Do you think if you never talk about those things that they'll somehow just fade away? It's my experience that they don't, Drake. I'm not saying that talking alone makes them easier to deal with, but at least it's a step in the right direction to making your peace with them.'

There was another irritated flash in his eyes, then he swallowed hard. 'The subject is closed. Closed as in you don't bring it up again…at least not until I indicate that you can. Is that clear?'

Mutely Layla nodded. It was definitely clear to her that now wasn't the time to try and delve deeper or prolong the discussion. And she didn't want to spoil their weekend together with a potentially heated argument. She would simply have to accept that she had to tread carefully round Drake until she sensed he was ready for a more intimate discourse about his past. Knowing he might *never* be ready for such a frank discussion, she either had to make her peace with that or walk away.

As he turned back towards the cooker she laid her hand just above his wrist, where a smattering of silken brown hair grazed the otherwise smooth flesh exposed by his rolled-up sweater sleeve. 'Why don't you let me cook the meal? You can pour yourself a nice glass of wine and go and relax in the living room. I'll come and get you when the food is ready.'

'As tempting as that sounds, you're my guest, remember?'

She couldn't help but grin. 'But I'm a very amiable guest, who doesn't mind mucking in when the situation calls for it. The fact that you're so tired definitely warrants my assistance. Go on…pour some wine and go and relax. I'll peer into cupboards and find out where everything is.'

Drake wrestled with her suggestion for just a couple of seconds longer, then relented. The troubled look on his face all but melted away before her eyes.

'You're the kind of guest that I could definitely get used to,' he teased, tipping up her chin and dropping a warm, sexy kiss that was far too fleeting onto her lips.

Layla knew if she slipped her hand behind his head to hold him there a little longer then all further discussion about food and cooking would be put on hold for quite some considerable time…

'Wait until you taste my food and see if you still think that.'

'Will you be okay using the cooker?' he checked.

'Good question.' She sighed, then grimaced as she scanned the large gleaming state-of-the-art hob and oven with its myriad chrome dials and knobs. 'I'm sure I'll be fine. It's an intimidating-looking beast, but surely

I don't need a degree in rocket science to fry a few shrimps and cook some rice…do I?'

Her handsome host chuckled. 'Let me turn on the hob for you.' He flicked a switch, turned a dial, and the hob underneath its black glass shield glowed instantly red. 'It's as easy and as straightforward as that. No degree in rocket science required. Think you'll be okay now?'

'Absolutely.'

'Good. I'll leave you to it, then. Would you like a glass of wine to enjoy while you're cooking?'

'As lovely as that sounds, I'd better not. I might put too much paprika or chilli in the mix, and if I get even the slightest bit intoxicated then our stir-fry will probably be inedible!'

'Warning received.'

Helping himself to a bottle from the sculpted metal rack on the other side of the room, along with a corkscrew and a glass, Drake left Layla with an irresistible lingering smile and a promise in his eyes that—if she let it—could tempt her away from the most sublime culinary feast even if she was starving…

CHAPTER SEVEN

He knew he'd had a lucky escape. But how long could he avoid talking about his past with a woman who made the walls of self-protection he'd carved round himself paper-thin every time she smiled into his eyes, let alone when he kissed her?

His elbows resting on his thighs, Drake stared blankly ahead of him at the glass of ruby-red wine he'd left languishing on the coffee table. He clasped his hands, unclasped them, then clasped them again. In a bid to divert his restlessness he got up and strode across the room to the music centre. When the familiar mournful voice of a male singer-songwriter filled the air he found himself honing in on the lyrics that echoed his own deep-rooted yearning for happiness and peace. Both those longed-for states had been way beyond his grasp ever-since he could remember.

Growing up in an atmosphere of tension and rage had very effectively seen to that. Even at the tender age of six Drake had intuitively understood why his mother had walked out on his father. He'd been a bitter, jealous, angry man who would have kept her under lock and key if he could. She'd had no life with him at all. Yet what Drake didn't understand—and probably never would—

was how she could have walked out on her defenceless son, leaving him with the brute she had married.

His hands reached up to his cheeks to scrub them roughly, as if by doing so he could delete the agonising memory from his mind and heart for ever. He *couldn't,* and his anguished thoughts ran on… How much resolve, faith and sheer grit had it taken for him to overcome his broken and unsupported childhood to reach the position he found himself in now? he asked himself.

Yes, he'd reached the heights of his profession, gained money and a laudable reputation beyond his wildest dreams, yet what good was any of it if at the end of his life he was still alone without someone to share it with? He released a slow harsh breath. With despair in her voice his ex had asked him the same question, and Drake had answered angrily.

'I'm not interested in marriage or having children. That's not for me. If you want that then you should go and find someone else.'

Well, Kirsty had taken him at his word and broken up with him that very night. Drake had heard recently through a mutual acquaintance that she was pregnant and engaged now, and he honestly wished her well. She was a nice woman, but not the soulmate he'd always secretly craved…a soulmate who would accept him for exactly who he was and not try to mould him into some imaginary ideal that she hoped he might become. What he wanted was a woman of infinite understanding with a capacity for unconditional love beyond measuring. It was a tall order.

Was Layla that woman?

Groaning out loud, he shook his head. How could

she be when she was already probing him with uncomfortable questions about his feelings and his past? All he wanted to do was enjoy her body and her company. He wasn't going to speculate much more beyond that. Shutting off the music, he returned to the luxuriously upholstered couch, reaching for his glass of wine and taking a long slug of the rich burgundy before his rear even touched the seat cushions.

Had he done the right thing leaving her to her own devices in the kitchen? he wondered.

His ensuing smile was helplessly wry. Her cooking surely couldn't be any worse than that of the incompetent housekeeper he'd recently let go. Layla worked in a café, for goodness' sake. She was well used to preparing food and making it look presentable. God forgive him, but he very much liked the idea of having her cook for him. In fact—despite his vow that he wouldn't speculate on the future—he very much liked the idea of having her around full-stop...

The shrimp stir-fry had worked out better than Layla had hoped, and she and Drake had finished every scrap. She had to admit that watching him tuck into a meal she'd prepared with such obvious relish had given her a real sense of satisfaction and pleasure—if only because her nervousness round him hadn't caused her to make a complete hash of it.

Immediately after they finished, she automatically stood up to clear the table, her intention to stack the dishwasher.

'Where do you think you're going?'

Although his grey eyes glinted with amusement, Drake's voice had a definitely irritated undertone.

'I was going to rinse the bowls and stack them in the dishwasher.'

'You don't think cooking a meal was more than enough demonstration of domesticity for one evening? Granted I need a housekeeper, but unless I've had a serious lapse of memory I wasn't aware that I'd given the position to you.'

'It's no big deal to clear up.'

'That's not why I invited you home with me.'

His rough-edged tone told her exactly why he'd invited her home, and Layla couldn't deny the same thought had been playing on her mind from the moment she'd set eyes on him back at his office…and even before that, when she'd somehow found herself packing a toothbrush and spare underwear into her tote. But she was still wary about surrendering to her physical desire for him too quickly. It was hard to shake the memory of how she'd been so badly used by her ex-boss.

'You invited me home with you because I presented you with a *fait accompli*, turning up at your office like that.' She stalled, crossing her arms over her chest. 'You probably felt obliged.'

'Obliged? You must be crazy.'

Abruptly getting to his feet, Drake strode round the glass-topped table. He unceremoniously pulled her against him, making her gasp. Suddenly Layla found herself on the most intimate of terms with his hard lean body, and the lust that blazed down at her from his eyes made her heart thump hard.

'I swear to God you've put a spell on me, woman—

because I can't think of anything else but having you in my bed.'

'You told me—you said that you had several guest rooms...that we didn't have to share a room tonight.' Her tongue was so thick she could barely get the words out.

'I must have fooled myself into believing that I had will power, then.'

At the precise moment he stopped talking Layla knew without a doubt that she was fighting a lost cause. Heat was already pouring through her body in a torrent of libidinous need that she could scarce contain, and the idea of spending the night alone in one of Drake's guest rooms instead of in his arms in his bed was akin to attempting to cross a burning hot desert without access to any drinking water. *She simply couldn't do it.*

'And I—I don't want to spend the night alone in one of your spare rooms, Drake.'

'Then come with me,' he husked.

Somehow, her hand held firmly in his, she found herself climbing another glass-lined staircase that led to an upper floor. Barely registering the lush oil paintings that hung here and there on the ivory-coloured walls, or the black velvet sky she glimpsed through the various windows they passed, now *she* was the one who felt as though she was under a spell. When they reached his bedroom she saw that it was an undoubtedly masculine retreat, with clean, uncluttered surfaces and an original restored oakwood floor without so much as a single rug covering even the smallest square of it. The only less than pristine note was the rumpled burgundy silk counterpane on the large king-size bed. It looked as though its owner had attempted to straighten it in a hurry, thought better of it, then irritably decided to just let it be.

Layla refused to entertain the idea that maybe it was rumpled because he'd spent the night in it with a lover. Such a possibility would ruin everything for her.

Briefly letting go of her hand, Drake touched his fingers to a dimmer switch on the wall next to the door and glowing lamps gently filled the room with softly intimate light. Then he closed the door behind them and, turning back, hungrily fastened his hands either side of her hips.

'Let me love you,' he breathed. 'No more talking or making promises we're afraid to keep in case they don't work out. Just let it be you and me alone together in this room…in this bed.'

He touched his lips to hers and the seductive spell already cast became a sensual magical dream that Layla never wanted to wake up from.

The hot thrust of his tongue into her mouth ignited a trail of fire straight to her core, causing her knees to buckle helplessly and making her sag as though drunk against the hard muscular wall of his chest. His arms immediately encircled her waist to hold her upright. Then she was effortlessly lifted up and transported across the room to the rumpled bed.

The moment she was lowered down onto the silken counterpane Layla knew it was imperative to get something off her chest before they went any further. 'I don't know what you've imagined, but I'm not—I'm not very experienced at this. The last occasion when I was intimate with someone was with my boss, and that was the most horrible mistake. Since then…' She screwed up her face. 'Since then I haven't even wanted to get close to a man like this.'

His grey eyes glinting with gentle amusement, Drake touched his palm to her cheek. 'I'm not interested in your past, Layla. The only thing I've imagined is you and me here and now, in this bed, writing a new page to both our histories.'

'I want that too, Drake… But, on the subject of histories, I need to ask has there—has there been anyone that's shared your bed lately?'

The astute grey eyes that seemed to be gifted with the unsettling ability to read her thoughts glinted with ironic disbelief, and perhaps some annoyance too. Layla sensed her cheeks redden helplessly. 'I haven't been intimate with anyone since my ex-girlfriend, and it's been six months since we broke up,' he confided.

'You didn't live together?'

'No. We did not.'

Easing out a relieved sigh, she ventured an apologetic smile. 'I didn't mean to embarrass you, but I had to know.'

'I understand.'

The steady, deeply assessing gaze he returned let her know he did indeed understand.

'Now that we know where we both stand, how about we go back to where we were?'

Feeling suddenly daring, and perhaps a little reckless too, Layla reached up to Drake to cup her hands round his iron jaw and pull his face down to hers. The lower half of his visage was already shaded with bristles, and they inevitably abraded her softer feminine skin as she seductively kissed him, inviting his equally seductive response. Their open-mouthed ravenous kissing quickly and inevitably built into another conflagration, and the passion and fervour that pulsed through Layla's veins secretly frightened her—because whatever came of this hot, wild attraction of theirs she already knew this man had ruined her for anyone else...

Tearing his mouth away from hers and breathing hard, Drake put out a hand and gently pushed her so that she found herself on her back. His silvery gaze searing her like a white-hot laser, he reached down and ripped the two sides of her cotton shirt apart so that the row of tiny buttons that fastened it flew off like confetti.

'I'll buy you a new one,' he murmured.

Before he could apply the same treatment to her front-fastening white lace bra, her heart thundering like a sprinter's as he raced for the finishing line, Layla deftly released the catch herself, so that her bared breasts were suddenly exposed to the silky night air and to her would-be lover's appreciative aroused glance.

'My God...you're even more beautiful than I imagined,' he declared, gravel-voiced.

Hurriedly assisting her to dispose of her torn shirt and bra, seconds later, with his well-developed jeans-clad thighs straddling her, Drake gave her the most intimately seductive smile she'd ever experienced. Then he bent his head to capture one of her tight aching nipples in the scalding cavern of his mouth. She almost hit the roof. The pleasure-pain as his teeth caught the tender flesh and lightly bit was like a lightning strike going straight to her womb. Moving his lips, he gave the same erotic treatment to its twin and, softly whimpering, Layla drove her fingers mindlessly through the silken strands of his hair to hold him to her.

Seconds later he came up for air and sat back on his heels. His hot, slumbrous gaze was filled with unashamed erotic intent, and slowly he unbuckled his leather belt, freed the button at the top of his jeans and unzipped his fly. 'You do the same,' he instructed huskily, at the same time reaching into his back pocket for a foil packet that he expertly ripped open.

Her mouth drying, Layla kicked off her shoes and, with fingers that shook helplessly, unzipped her jeans. Taking hold of both sides, she momentarily lifted her bottom up off the bed so that she could push the heavy denim down over her thighs. In front of her, Drake took the opportunity to discard his own clothing and expertly sheathed his aroused manhood with the latex protection. Her blood pounded with primal need when she saw the sheer magnificence of his strong and proud male body, with toned, well-defined muscles and a flat, lean abdomen. His job might not be physically demanding, but he clearly didn't avoid the necessity to keep himself fit and strong.

Before Layla could rid herself completely of the jeans she had pushed down her legs Drake took over the task with a definitely urgent air, and straight afterwards tugged her silk white panties over her slender hips and jettisoned them carelessly over his shoulder. Bending towards her, he claimed her lips in a crushing hot kiss that not only stole her breath but acted like a seismic eruption in her already overheated blood. He was still kissing her when she felt his hand reach down to firmly press her thighs apart and brush once, twice, three times over her sensitive feminine core. The pleasure that intimate caress instigated was so intense that, because he was still kissing her, she had to swallow the low moan that immediately threatened to surface. But when he suddenly drove himself deeply inside her in a possessive motion that bordered on the passionately rough Layla freed her lips from his to gasp her shock and pleasure out loud against his shoulder.

She wasn't a virgin, but apart from the unfortunate encounter with her ex-boss she hadn't had sex for a long time, and her feminine muscles were tighter than she'd imagined they would be. Consequently she felt every exquisite inch of her lover. And now, even though there was no question that Drake desired and wanted her, insecurity surfaced. She had so little experience in knowing how to please a man. What if their love-making didn't live up to his expectations? What if she disappointed him?

Seconds later both those unhelpful thoughts flew instantly from her mind as he started to move faster and more rhythmically inside her and she automatically wrapped her arms round his strongly corded neck to hold on. Making love with Drake was like riding the most tumultuous exhilarating wave, Layla thought.

As the inflammatory silkily hot sensations building inside her went way beyond the point where she could control them she dug her fingernails into his hard-muscled back and cried out as wave after wave of erotic velvet heat consumed her. With a deep guttural groan, and the light lustre of perspiration standing out on his handsome forehead, Drake suddenly stilled, and she knew that he too had reached the sensual pinnacle of their impassioned union.

Her heart leapt when he didn't immediately move away, as she'd thought he might. Instead he leant forward and, with his face just bare inches from hers—so close that she could almost count every lustrous dark eyelash that swept over his dazzling silver gaze—said, 'You may not have a lot of experience, my angel, but when it comes to satisfying a man's desire, trust me— you have everything that's needed and much more besides.' He finished this comment with a sexy boyish grin that all but stopped her heart.

'You're not so bad yourself.' She smiled.

After dropping a warm and lazy kiss on her surprised mouth, he lay down with his head between her breasts and trailed his fingers gently up and down her bare arm. Revelling in his deliciously erotic male scent, and the weight of his hard, lean body pressing her firmly down into the mattress, Layla resolved to memorise every moment of this ardent union with Drake— knowing that whatever happened to her in the future she would never forget it…

The second time they made love that night it was no less passionate, but the caresses on both sides were infused with tenderness and much more considered. To Layla's delight, Drake paid particular attention to ensuring she received just as much pleasure and satisfaction as he did—if not more—and in turn she loved the fact that her intuition and desire led her to discovering just where and how he liked to be touched. In that discovery all her doubts about knowing how to please him disappeared.

Afterwards, they fell asleep in each other's arms in the softly illuminated lamplit room.

After waking in the middle of the night because she was in need of the bathroom, Layla quickly returned to the sumptuous dishevelled bed she had so briefly vacated and switched off the lamps on the gleaming walnut cabinets that stood either side of it. The room was plunged into a near pitch-black darkness that was punctuated by the sound of Drake's gentle breathing. He appeared to be in the deepest of slumbers.

Pleased at the thought that their lovemaking had helped him to relax, she snuggled down beside him, gently laid her arm across his abdomen and closed her eyes.

What could have been no more than a few minutes later, she found her arm violently pushed aside with an anguished shout.

'Drake, what is it?' Her hand quickly fumbling for the light switch on the lamp next to her, Layla pushed up into a sitting position as once again the room was suffused with a softly diffused glow.

Hearing the laboured breathing of the man lying by her side, she saw with a start that his brow was studded with perspiration, almost as though he was sweating out a fever. When he turned his head to look at her she saw that his wide-eyed gaze was nothing less than terrified. In the depths of his haunted grey eyes she saw the pain and horror of a man who had been shown a devastating glimpse of hell and believed himself to be trapped in that realm, perhaps for ever.

Leaning towards him, she cautiously touched his shoulder, softly murmuring, 'You must have had a nightmare…a bad dream. But it's gone now, Drake. You're safe and here with me. There's nothing to worry about, I promise.'

In response, he shrugged off her hand and roughly drove his fingers through his hair. Then he sat up. After that he simply fell into a kind of stunned trance, remaining mute. His harsh breaths continued for several more seconds before eventually returning to a more regular rhythm.

Still staring straight ahead of him he spoke. And his voice sounded as if it scraped over gravel when he declared suddenly, 'You turned out the lights.'

Tugging the silk counterpane protectively up over her breasts, Layla felt inexplicable fear wash over her like an icy river. The statement had sounded like an accusation. 'I did it automatically…when I returned from the bathroom.'

'I don't sleep with the lights out…*ever*.'

'I'm sorry. I didn't know that. If it makes things more comfortable for you, I can sleep in one of your guest rooms for the rest of the night, if you like?'

The scowl on his handsome face as he turned towards her was forbidding. 'No! I don't want that.'

Layla's blood ran cold for a second time. 'All right, then, I'll—I'll stay here with you.'

'I'm sorry, Layla. I'm sorry if I scared you.' He grimaced.

'It must have been a terrible dream. Do you think that you could tell me about it?'

Although his troubled expression had started to ease

a little, Drake stared at her as if once again cornered by something frighteningly threatening. 'Please don't ask me. It's not something I feel ready to share and I don't know if I ever will.'

'This is one of those places you don't want me to go? Is that what you're telling me?'

He nodded and looked desolate for a moment, and although she desperately wanted to know Layla knew this wasn't the time to enquire more deeply into why he didn't sleep with the lights off. What he needed right now was unquestioning understanding, she decided, and maybe some consolation as well. Nightmares could disturb the strongest of characters.

Pushing aside the silk counterpane, she moved towards him, cupped his jaw, then tenderly kissed him on the mouth. It was like touching flame to dry tinder, and straight away the heat that flared between them made him haul her onto his lap so that her thighs spread over his, and the clash of lips, teeth and tongues became even more urgent and demanding.

When Drake moved his hands to her hips to position her over his already hard member, then pushed up inside her, Layla threw back her head and let loose a deep throated groan. She was still a little tender from their previous energetic coupling, but in a way this raw and elemental coming together was even more inevitable and necessary than both those occasions— because right now Drake really *needed* her. And for the first time in her life she discovered that she finally knew what it was to really need a man too…

As he started to move more deeply inside her his palms hungrily cupped and kneaded her breasts. Every now and then his fingers and thumbs tugged at her rigid nipples, sending fiery heat directly to her womb. With her tousled dark hair falling around her face Layla stared back into his blazing lustful glance, her heart pounding so hard it was difficult to think straight. But most of all she was struck dumb by the sheer intensity of the feelings she saw reflected in his eyes.

'You are one seriously sexy and beautiful woman,' he declared huskily, his breathing ragged with unashamed need and desire.

Leaving her breasts, his hands reached up to pull her face down to his. Just as their lips made contact she sensed him buck beneath her, and even as he kissed her it was with a mixture of shock and pleasure that she registered the hot liquid heat that spurted into her womb. But there was barely time to contemplate the event because in the very next moment her own climax burst upon her. Freeing her lips from his still demanding mouth and oh-so-seductive moist tongue, she let her head fall against Drake's hard-muscled shoulder with a breathless gasp that was quickly followed by several more...

CHAPTER EIGHT

LAYLA was taking a shower and washing her hair. Having left her with one of his finest cotton shirts to replace the pretty blouse he had ripped open last night, Drake had nipped out to a local French *patisserie* to buy warm croissants and a pot of speciality fruit jam for them to enjoy with their morning coffee. Even as his mind teemed with provocative detailed reruns of the events of last night his body throbbed from the passionate lovemaking they had shared. He'd had little sleep, God knew, but this morning he felt on top of the world.

But as he let himself back inside the house, then made his way into the kitchen, it hit him like a steel wave crashing into his gut—how he had awoken in the suffocating dark and for chilling seconds been plunged back into the nightmare of his childhood.

Reaching for the kettle, he witnessed his hand shake slightly and cursed furiously. He still didn't know why Layla hadn't pressed him more for an explanation. Under the circumstances she'd had a perfect right to. What must she have thought when he'd told her that he never slept without the lights on?

He caught his breath when he remembered what she had done instead of probing him for answers. With her beautiful body moving over him, taking him to heaven instead of hell, Drake had quickly forgotten his nightmare of being locked in his bedroom in the dark and then hearing the slamming of the door that told him his father had gone out to the pub.

Even when his father had returned he'd never come up to unlock his son's door or check if he was okay. No, Drake would be forced to stay there until he'd cried himself to sleep.

Needing to shake off the hurt that suffused him at the memory, he filled the kettle from a filtered water jug and pressed the switch for it to boil. Then he measured generous spoonsful of aromatic coffee grounds into a cafetière and arranged the warm croissants he'd bought on two patterned side plates. As he reached into the fridge for some milk, another disturbing realisation stopped him in his tracks. Instead of cursing, this one made him shut the fridge door dazedly and stand there shaking his head in wonder and disbelief.

Caught up in the vortex of uncontrollable need and lust last night, along with the fantasy that maybe Layla was the woman who really *could* help put an end to his nightmares and loneliness for good, if she genuinely grew to care for him, he hadn't given a thought to using protection. And, having not had sex for a long time until her boss had so deviously seduced her by plying her with drink, he doubted very much that Layla was on the pill. In which case it was entirely possible that Drake had made her pregnant. If such event occurred then it was the most reckless act he'd committed since he'd left his teenage years behind and become a man.

'Hello, again… Are you making coffee, by any chance?'

Standing in the doorway with a shaft of sunlight playing upon her newly washed dark hair, wearing Drake's too-large pristine white shirt over fitted blue jeans, his ravishing lover took his breath away. It struck him that he'd never seen a woman look more beautiful or desirable as Layla did right then.

As he moved towards her his heart skipped a beat. 'Hi. Not only am I making coffee, but I've been out to buy us some croissants and fruit preserve too.'

Walking into his arms as though it was the most natural thing in the world for her to do, she teased, 'You must be trying to win the Most Considerate Man of the Year award, then. Don't worry, as far as I'm concerned you've already won the prize.' Reaching up and kissing him on the mouth, she glanced up at him from beneath her lustrous dark lashes and blushed charmingly.

Drake chuckled. 'Ain't that the truth…? I certainly *have* won the prize.' As his arms tightened a little more round her slender hourglass waist, he smiled. 'By the way, I'm never going to wash that shirt of mine again when you give it back.'

'Why?'

'Because it will have the scent of your very sexy body all over it… From now on it's elevated to being my favourite item of clothing.'

'Well, on that rather provocative little note, I think we should sit down and partake of those delicious-looking croissants you've bought…of course that's as soon as you get your act together and make the coffee, Mr Ashton,' she added mischievously.

As she extricated herself from his arms to move towards the table he caught hold of her hand and, lifting it to his lips, reverently kissed her fingers.

'What was that for?'

'Do I need a reason other than that I simply felt like it?' Feeling his heart swell with the kind of addictive warmth he couldn't ever remember feeling before, Drake kept a hold of Layla's hand, reluctant to let it go. 'That's not strictly true. I just wanted to thank you for last night…for understanding.'

It was a relief to him to know that he didn't have to say any more than that, because staring back into her compassionate brown eyes he knew no other explanation was necessary…at least for now.

'I hated seeing you so distressed. Whatever horrors you were dreaming about, I just wanted to try and help you forget them.'

'Trust me…' He grinned. 'You did.'

As he released her hand so he could return to the counter and make the coffee Layla frowned and briefly touched his arm, indicating that she wanted to extend their little discussion. 'Drake?'

'What is it?'

'Last night when we—when we made love again… we didn't use protection.'

'I was standing here thinking about that just before you came in.' He rubbed his hand round his chiselled jaw and grimaced. 'I'm usually much more careful about such things, but I'm afraid that the power of events rendered my common sense obsolete.' As if subconsciously illustrating the fact, he moved his heated glance helplessly up and down her figure. 'I definitely wasn't thinking straight, that's for sure. It's understandable that you've been worrying yourself sick.'

'What happened wasn't just down to you, Drake.' Shrugging a rueful shoulder, Layla nonetheless made her gaze direct as she levelled it at him. 'You weren't the only one who wasn't thinking straight. But I'm going to have to find the nearest chemist when we've finished our breakfast, so that I can buy an emergency contraceptive pill.'

Drake didn't know why, but a deeply unsettled feeling swept through him. If he had to analyse it he'd probably describe it as a sense of indignant protest… as if something he hadn't even known was precious was being threatened and being taken away from him.

'Anyway, I'll have my breakfast and then head out and find a chemist. Do you know if there's one nearby?'

Clenching his jaw a little, he answered soberly, 'There is. Don't worry. I'll take you there.'

'Thanks.' Lowering her glance, she wrapped her arms protectively round her chest, as though perturbed. Then she silently made her way over to the table and sat down.

Right then Drake couldn't find the courage to ask her why she suddenly looked so sad…

The day was surprisingly fair, and they agreed to kick off their weekend break with a visit to one of the capital's well-known art galleries. They were running separate exhibitions by two influential British artists whose work Layla and Drake both admired and were keen to view. But as they walked slowly through the lofty wooden-floored galleries with the same reverential sense of visitors to a hushed cathedral, the morning-after pill that Layla had purchased from the chemist all but burned a guilty hole in her coat pocket.

Between them they seemed to have made an unspoken agreement not to discuss the topic again, and certainly Drake hadn't suggested she take the contraceptive straight away. It was probably utter madness, and Layla didn't know why she should be so hesitant in swallowing the pill with the mineral water she'd purchased. Except that if she was really honest with herself she *did* know why. Since last night her heart had been full of a passionate romantic longing she couldn't seem to control, and as she walked round the gallery with her hand firmly encased in her handsome companion's it just grew stronger and stronger.

What would it be like to be the mother of this enigmatic man's child? she wondered. Would he adore his son or daughter as much as Layla undoubtedly knew she would? There was still so much about Drake that she didn't know—places that he'd warned her to stay away from… It had crossed her mind more than once today that the nightmare he'd had last night probably involved some disturbing memories from his past. *What were they?* He'd told her yesterday that he hadn't known much joy in the house where he'd grown up, only sorrow. If only she could persuade him to share some of the experiences that haunted him it might help dispel the hold they had on him.

Stopping in front of a jolting 'warts and all' self-portrait of the artist whose work they were viewing, Layla stared back into bottomless blue eyes that seemed so full of pain and regret and desires left unfulfilled and expelled a helpless sigh of commiseration.

Turning his head to study her, Drake was immediately concerned. 'What's wrong?'

'He looks like such a tormented soul, bless him.'

'By all accounts he was. A latter-day Van Gogh who was plagued by depression and eventually took his own life. But at least while he lived he did what he loved.'

'I suppose we should thank God for small mercies. Do you still love what *you* do, Drake?'

'Of course.'

There was no hesitation in his answer, and Layla was pleased that at least there was one area of his life where unhappiness and a sense of isolation didn't dog him as she was beginning to guess it often did. 'Did you ever do any drawing or painting as a child?' she asked conversationally.

A shadow immediately stole across his face. 'Only when I was at school.'

'And did you enjoy it?'

A corner of his mouth quirked, nudging an engaging dimple in the side of his cheek and dispelling the shadow she'd glimpsed. 'I did. Turns out that I had a bit of a talent for it... I guess it was the precursor of my love of designing houses—which is why I chose architecture as a career. I suppose, as well, I always believed that our homes should be beautiful, and if I designed them I could make them as beautiful as I wanted.'

'That's a lovely intention. You never drew or dabbled with paints at home?'

'No.'

It was a flat no, without any suggestion or possibility of further elucidation, Layla realised.

'Didn't you want to?' she ventured.

Her companion stayed worryingly silent.

'Clearly this must be another one of those places that I'm not supposed to go, then?' She couldn't prevent the note of exasperation that crept into her voice.

He lifted a dark eyebrow and lightly shook his head. 'My home-life was hardly conducive to having the freedom to draw or experiment with paint or colour. That's all I'll tell you for the time being. Perhaps we can talk about this later? Right now I think we should just enjoy the art, don't you? After all, it's what we came for.'

Although Drake's response might not be as warm as she could wish, it did stir a faint hope in her that at last he was coming round to the idea of discussing his past with her.

For some reason all of a sudden she couldn't abide the thought of the all-important pill burning a hole in her pocket. What was she *thinking* of, delaying taking it? She wasn't an immature teenager, for goodness' sake! She was a fully-grown woman and the situation called for her to be sensible and realistic.

What on earth had possessed her to become so entranced by the crazy notion of having Drake's baby? They weren't in a committed relationship. She worked in a low-paid job in a café, and Drake had an important commission to help regenerate their underachieving impoverished town and help set it on its feet again. The last thing he or she needed was to be faced with the prospect of having a baby. Add to this the fact that they'd only known each other for the shortest time, and this sizzling sexual heat they had for each other would likely burn itself out very soon, and it simply confirmed that her decision to take the damn pill was absolutely the right one. Anything else was simply delusional... perhaps *dangerously* so.

Yet it didn't help the ache in Layla's heart whenever she so much as glanced at Drake to become any less intense.

Glancing round, she saw the sign for the ladies' room at the far end of the gallery and, abruptly freeing her hand from his clasp, murmured, 'Excuse me, but I need to go to the Ladies. I won't be long.'

'Layla?' His grey eyes glinted with such concern that it made her insides execute a cartwheel.

'Yes?'

'Are you okay?'

'Yes, I'm fine.'

'When you get back we'll go upstairs to the restaurant and get some coffee. After we've seen everything we want to see here I'd like to take you shopping, to buy a new blouse to replace the one I ripped.'

'There's no need.' Scalding heat poured into her cheeks at the memory of just *how* he had managed to rip her blouse, and as if he'd read her mind Drake's grey eyes twinkled in amusement.

'Yes, there is,' he argued with a husky catch in his voice. 'I want my shirt back.'

She knew he was trying to make amends for his curt tone earlier, and while it warmed her to think that he cared about her feelings, and about replacing the blouse he'd torn in the heat of passion last night, she couldn't deny that she suddenly felt unspeakably desolate at the idea that other than sexually he probably wasn't going to let her get anywhere *near* the wounded man she guessed hid behind the self-contained façade of wealth and success he projected after all. She was feeling less and less sure he really would discuss his past with her.

'Okay. We'll have coffee, see the rest of the exhibition, then go shopping.' Turning away, she headed briskly towards the end of the gallery without checking even once to see if his mercurial haunting gaze followed her progress...

By the time she emerged from the ladies' room Layla had sat in the toilet cubicle breaking her heart for at least ten minutes. Then, when she'd calmed down sufficiently to realise the utter futility of her behaviour, she'd stepped out in front of the bank of unforgiving bathroom mirrors to find her eye make-up tellingly smudged and her face as white as a ghost's. After re-applying her make-up and spritzing the inside of her wrists with the last of her perfume—a precious leftover luxury from her time working in London—she'd finally swallowed the contraception down with at least half a bottle of water, tossed back her hair, lifted her chin and returned to the gallery to find Drake.

She spied him sitting on one of the long wooden benches interspersed here and there in front of the displayed paintings. With his hands loosely linked across his knees and his neck bent because he was staring down at the floor, it wasn't hard to deduce that he wasn't meditating on the stunning art. No, once again he was lost in a compelling world of his own.

'Drake?'

'You're back.'

Layla was dumbfounded by the relief and delight in his eyes. Giving her a smile more precious to her right then than all the world's diamonds, he stood up and gathered her into his arms. Transfixed, she felt as if the priceless art along with every single soul in the gallery simply disappeared. All she could focus on right then were the carved masculine lips that slowly but surely moved towards hers to greet her with an all too brief but hungry kiss. The velvet touch of his mouth and the delicious sensation of his strong arms urging her against him were a powerful antidote to the distressing doubt and fear that had accompanied her to the ladies' room.

As Drake lifted his head to glance down at her she smiled and asked, 'Did you think I wasn't coming back?'

'You were gone a long time. I was getting worried.'

'Well, there was no need.' Seeing by his expression that he wasn't convinced, she felt her heart skip a beat. 'What were you worrying about? Did you think I'd slipped out the back way and abandoned you?' she teased.

'Don't joke about something like that.'

Immediately Layla saw that her unfortunately phrased question had touched a raw nerve and she winced in remorse. 'I meant nothing by it—honestly.'

A searching look crept into his eyes. Lowering his voice he asked, 'Did you take that pill?'

'Yes…I did.'

He stared back at her as if totally at a loss to know what to say.

'It's all right,' she assured him hurriedly. 'It was the right thing to do…the *only* thing.'

'Of course it was.'

'Is there something about what happened between us that you'd like to talk about?'

'What else is there to say?'

'I suppose there's plenty to say if you're willing to be more open about your feelings. You said you'd let me get to know you, remember? I can't help worrying about how I'm going to accomplish that if you keep on blocking every single avenue I try to go down.'

He dropped his arms from round her waist and folded them across his chest instead—across the sky-blue cashmere sweater he wore beneath his stylishly battered black leather jacket. 'I know you're not going to like my answer, but this really isn't the ideal venue for a frank and personal discussion. Why don't we wait until we get back to my place and talk about things then, like I suggested?'

Her heart thudding, once again Layla felt infused with hope. 'You mean it? You'll really talk to me openly and frankly and not refuse to answer any questions you're uncomfortable with? To reassure you—I'm not some unscrupulous reporter who wants to write tittle-tattle about your life, Drake... I—I really care about you.'

'Do you?'

It hurt her heart that there was suspicion amid the flare of hope she detected in his eyes. 'Of course I do. Why do you think I chose to come up to London of my own accord to see you? Also, in spite of the stupid mistake I made with my boss, I'm not in the habit of having one-night stands. I slept with you because it meant something to me...don't you know that?' She stole a quick glance round to check they weren't being overheard.

Drake's broad shoulders lifted in a shrug, and the slight flush beneath his carved cheekbones illustrated his discomfort at the highly personal turn their conversation had taken. 'Okay… I'll agree to be as candid with you as I can,' he relented, 'but only if you respect that talking about my life and my feelings isn't a muscle I flex easily. If any particularly difficult areas come up, I don't want you to be aggrieved or to take it personally if I don't feel I can discuss them.'

In answer, Layla caught and held one of the large smooth hands with its callused forefinger and thumb that were testimony that he didn't shy away from hard physical work as well as more artistic and creative pursuits. 'I'm not the Spanish Inquisition, Drake. If there are things you really don't feel able to discuss then of course I'll respect that. And, just so that we're even, I promise to answer any questions you want to ask about *me*…deal?'

Raising a gently mocking eyebrow, he draped his arm affectionately round her shoulders and pulled her into his side. 'Now I know where the phrase "she who must be obeyed" comes from,' he joked.

CHAPTER NINE

BEFORE they went home Drake took Layla to an exclusive boutique in Mayfair to buy her a new blouse. From the moment he selected the shop to the minute they walked through the door he could sense her growing uneasiness with the project. He couldn't understand why she seemed so reticent. There wasn't one single woman he was acquainted with who didn't like shopping. But then he already knew that Layla was unique. She was constantly surprising him.

The wafer-thin blonde assistant in her short-skirted dogtooth suit lit up like a hundred-watt lightbulb when they entered. Whether or not that was because she scented that Drake had money, he didn't particularly care, so long as Layla was satisfied she'd acquired a blouse she was pleased with and would wear.

When, at his urging, she reluctantly started to examine the exquisite silk blouses on the very selective display rails and picked practically the first item she looked at, as if she couldn't wait to get out of the shop, Drake shook his head with a teasing smile.

'Do you really want that one?' he asked doubtfully, privately thinking how prim and proper the elegant white garment appeared, even if it *was* made from the finest French silk crêpe.

'I don't want you to buy me one at all, if I'm honest.' Layla sighed, self-consciously brushing her hair back with her hand. 'I'm quite happy to wear your shirt until I get home.'

'But you're not going home until tomorrow, remember?'

'Then you can lend me another shirt tomorrow. I'm sure you must own more than one.'

Her caramel-brown eyes sparkled with a mixture of defiance and merriment, and for a long moment Drake was transfixed by the heated longing that gripped him. It struck him like a thunderbolt right then that he was quite simply crazy about her, and almost couldn't bear the thought of having her out of his sight. Excepting the mother who had deserted him, he'd never needed *anyone* that much before. The feeling was terrifying and exhilarating all at the same time…

He levelled his glance. 'As great as my shirt looks on you, I'd really like to buy something exclusively for *you*…something pretty and sexy that will make you think of me every time you wear it next to your skin.'

He was rewarded with the most bewitching and pretty blush.

'You choose something for me then,' she suggested softly.

He didn't miss the slight catch in her voice that told him she'd definitely been aroused by what he'd said. With an undeniable sense of satisfying male pride, and only too happy to oblige, Drake selected a couple of much more delicate specimens, made from what was labelled 'silk Charmeuse' and handed them to her.

'They're far too flimsy,' she protested, dark eyes widening. 'They look more like lingerie.'

'Then they're just what we're looking for,' he taunted gently.

'They are?'

'Trust me—you're going to have the most appreciative audience you can imagine when you wear them.'

The smooth skin between Layla's elegant dark brows creased a little. 'I only need one blouse, Drake, not two.' Leaning towards him, she lowered her voice to a near whisper. 'Have you seen the prices on these?' Turning the labels that were so prettily attached to the garments with slim pink and blue ribbons towards him, she seemed intent on his noting them.

He didn't even trouble to spare them a glance. Instead he chuckled, then tenderly cupped her delicate jaw in the palm of his hand. 'That's the last thing you need to worry about, angel... And I'm not about to apologise for having money just because it makes you uncomfortable either.'

Her lips curved in a conciliatory smile. 'Okay, I'll go and try them on. Seeing as you've picked them out, it would be rude not to. Besides, it's very hard to refuse you anything when you look at me like that,' she breathed.

'How *am* I looking at you? Tell me.'

'Like I'm the gourmet meal you've been anticipating enjoying all day.'

With a provocative grin that sent the blood in Drake's

veins plunging helplessly south, she spun round on her heel and politely asked the assistant to show her to the changing room.

As Drake returned to the living room and placed the two cups of coffee he'd made down on the carved Regency table positioned in front of the sofa, Layla smiled up at him, commenting, 'Mmm…just what the doctor ordered after that great spaghetti you rustled up for dinner.' Curling her hair round her ear, her expression pensive, she added, 'Come and sit down.'

'I was intending on doing exactly that.'

'We've had a wonderful day together, haven't we?'

'We have indeed.'

She fell silent for a few moments, then said, 'Drake?'

'What's on your mind?'

'Do you think we could have that talk of ours now?'

Momentarily distracted by the very feminine ivory-silk blouse she now wore in place of his white shirt, noting as he'd done at dinner that the sheer material meant he could see right through it to the pretty lace bra she had on underneath, Drake didn't immediately register her question. When the words finally sank in his stomach plunged to his boots. Clearly there weren't going to be any preliminaries to this little discussion of theirs, and it was becoming worryingly clear that he wasn't going to be able to hide the truth of his past from her any longer.

His skin prickled hotly, and for one sickeningly uncomfortable moment he felt akin to a cornered animal. Raking his fingers through his hair, he dropped down onto the pinstriped armchair at the other side of the table, resting his forearms on his jeans-clad thighs with a heavy sigh.

'So what do you want to talk about? My favourite music? Or maybe you'd like to hear what my top ten favourite movies are?' He was hedging for time, using humour as a shield to divert any immediately awkward or difficult questions. But when he saw the concerned frown on Layla's beautiful face Drake felt oddly guilty for taking such a cowardly tack.

'Whilst I'd love to know what music you like, also what your favourite movies are, right now I'd like you to tell me a bit more about yourself. Then, as I said before...you can ask me things too.'

Linking his hands, he locked his glance with hers in a deliberately challenging stare. 'Then why don't you ask me a direct question and I'll endeavour to answer it?'

'All right, then.' She nervously licked her lips and curled her hair round her ear again. 'I'd like you to tell me a bit about your childhood.'

'What would you like to know, exactly?'

'Was it hard for you, being an only child?'

'Compared to what? Being one of a large brood? How would I know, since that wasn't my experience?'

'Okay, then, perhaps you'll tell me instead what it was like for you growing up in the area?'

It was the question Drake had feared the most, but he resolved himself to answer it because he didn't want Layla to believe even for a second that he lacked the courage to tell her.

'What was it like? In two words...miserable and lonely.' Moving his head from side to side, he clasped and unclasped his hands. 'I had a mother whose mind was always on leaving, and a father who was a bully and a drunk. After she left his bullying moved up to a whole new level. You can't imagine how creative he could be when it came to devising punishments for me. Consequently I was always dreaming of ways to escape. When my art teacher at school took a serious interest in my ability for drawing and design, and suggested I might try to become an architect, I latched onto the possibility as though it was a lifeline—which indeed it was. From that moment on I didn't care what my father did to me, because I knew that one day I'd get away… I'd carve a whole new life for myself and escape from both him *and* our drab little town for good.'

'So how did you do that? Did you get the grades to go to university?'

'Yes. I worked damned hard and fortunately I did.'

'Did you see your father at all after you went?' As she took a sip of her coffee, then carefully set the blue and white cup back in its elegant saucer, Layla's dark-eyed glance was thoughtful.

'No.' In return, Drake's smile was helplessly bitter. 'I only returned once after I left, and that was to go to his funeral. Needless to say I was the only mourner. Let's put it this way: he wasn't the most popular guy in the world.'

'So how did he die? What happened to him?'

'The silly fool smashed into a central reservation on the motorway whilst driving under the influence of alcohol. He was killed outright.' Drake agitatedly tunnelled his fingers back and forth through his hair. 'It wasn't even his car. He'd borrowed it from some drink-

ing crony who stupidly believed he'd return it in one
piece. When I talked to the man he told me that my
father was planning on driving up to the university to
visit me. That's why he'd borrowed the car. Unless he'd
had some profound religious conversion and wanted to
atone for his past ill-treatment of me, I very much doubt
that it was true.'

'My God, Drake!'

Layla's expression was almost distraught, he saw.
Knowing her kind heart, it wouldn't have surprised
him to learn that she was feeling compassion for his
loser of a father.

'I'm so sorry you had to face such a horrendous
and sad ordeal on your own,' she murmured, twisting
her hands together in her lap. 'It must have been hard
enough for you not to have someone back at home, sending you love and support while you were away studying,
but then to hear that your father had died…and possibly
on his way to visit you as well…?'

'You think it was *hard* for me, do you?' he challenged, his temper rising. The old, painful wounds that
he privately nursed, encrusted with bitterness and resentment, were still apt to make him feel murderous.
'The only thing I felt when I heard the bastard had died
was relief like you can't possibly imagine!'

'You said he was cruel. Was his cruelty the reason
you don't like sleeping without the light on?'

Sensing all the colour drain from his face, Drake
shivered hard at the haunting reminder of his appalling
home-life when he was a boy. 'Every night he'd remove
the lightbulbs in my bedroom and lock me in for the
night in the dark. More often than not he'd go out and

leave me on my own until the early hours of the morning, and even when he returned he wouldn't knock on my door to check and see if I was all right.'

'Why? Why did he do that?'

Drake's lips twisted in disgust. 'He told me it would make me a man. Personally, I think he did it simply because he *could*.'

'You should have reported him...told someone at your school what he was doing. That kind of inhuman behaviour is child abuse, Drake.'

'You make it sound so simple—but how does a frightened child tell someone his private horror story when he feels the most sickening shame about it? When he secretly believes he must have done something bad to deserve it?'

'You did nothing wrong. You were only a little boy, for goodness' sake! Your father was the adult in the family. He should have taken proper care of you. You aren't supposed to "deserve" love and care. It's the fundamental right of human children everywhere. I wish someone could have told you that so you wouldn't have carried such shame and fear around with you all these years.'

'Well, they didn't, and I managed. End of story.'

'You may have managed to get by despite your circumstances, but that's not the end of the story, Drake... not if you're still afraid to sleep in the dark and are plagued with nightmares.'

'That's not your concern. I deal with it. Shall we change the subject?'

'I've one more question. Do you mind?'

Before Layla got the chance to ask it, he interjected

quickly, feeling bleak. 'I *do* mind, as I'm sure you know, but ask anyway. Then it's my turn.'

'What about your mother, Drake?'

Her luminous dark eyes were tender and her tone was infinitely gentle, respectful of the now tense atmosphere between them...like an intrepid novice explorer negotiating the walk across a frozen river for the very first time. One false move could make the ice splinter and send her plunging into the freezing waters below.

'Did you ever see her again after she left?'

'No, I didn't. She obviously just wanted to put her seven years with my father behind her—start a new life somewhere else and forget about us both.'

'Why would she want to forget about her little son? I'm sure that can't be true, Drake. Her heart must have been breaking in two to leave you behind with a man like your father. She must have been absolutely desperate for her to carry out such an act.'

He gulped down some of his coffee, then wiped the back of his hand across his mouth. 'Desperate or not, she presumably made a better life for herself somewhere else and decided not to risk ruining it by coming back for me.'

Restlessly he pushed to his feet, absolutely hating the misery and pain that made him feel unbearably exposed and vulnerable in front of a woman he already cared too much about. A woman whose rejection of him, if it ever came, he would probably never recover from. For a few desperate moments he despised Layla for the power she unknowingly held over him. He was also furious with her for goading him into revisiting the tormented past he'd striven so hard to forget.

Before he knew it, Drake had turned on her with a fierce scowl. 'Are you happy now? What else do you want to know about me so that you can sit there smugly making your analysis? An analysis that will no doubt help you feel *so* much better about your own comparatively trivial disappointments.'

Stricken, Layla rose slowly to her feet and folded her arms over the pretty diaphanous blouse Drake had taken such pleasure in seeing her wearing. 'We're not having a competition about who's suffered the most, Drake. All I wanted to do…all I *hoped* to do was get to know you a little, so that you wouldn't feel the need to be anyone other than yourself…your *real* self…around me. Yes, we've all had sadness and disappointment in our lives—and some of us, like you, have experienced dreadfully unhappy childhoods… But that doesn't mean we should be ashamed of our pasts or try to hide them. Sometimes it's our most challenging and difficult experiences that help us evolve into the compassionate and thoughtful people we are.'

'Is that how you felt when your unscrupulous exboss fleeced you of your life savings…*compassionate*?'

Hearing the almost cruel mockery in Drake's tone, Layla hugged her arms over her chest even more, needing to protect herself. *Had she pushed him too far and too soon in getting him to talk about his past?* What if her kindly meant questioning to get him to open up a little about himself so that they might forge a closer bond had done nothing but turn him against her and made him suspicious of her motives? If they didn't have trust then they had nothing worth having at all.

'No,' she replied. 'I didn't feel remotely compassionate towards him. I was too busy blaming him for cheating me and blaming myself for being an idiot for trusting him in the first place…for being so gullible in trusting my savings to his little scheme and for letting him seduce me.'

'He got you drunk.'

Unhappily she nodded her head. 'Yes, but I let him. I could have said no to him, but he was a charmer and I fell under his spell. Anyway, that aside, after some time had gone by I definitely felt as though I'd learned a lesson I'd never forget. For a start, I'd have loved to give the money I had to Marc, to help the business. As for my boss, I know that if he carries on cheating people like he does then inevitably life will teach *him* an invaluable lesson. A lesson that will hopefully make him reflect on his behaviour and stop him seeking to advance himself by exploiting anyone else.' She chewed thoughtfully down on her lip, then smiled uncertainly. 'At least that's my hope.'

Drake started to pace the polished wooden floor, the expression in his fascinating grey eyes suggesting they were reaching internally for some longed-for escape route…perhaps a time warp that could transport them back to the moment when he'd first walked into the room with their coffee, when he might have told Layla he'd changed his mind about having their little discussion.

All her instincts cried out for her to go to him and hold him tight, to tell him how courageous he'd been to reveal the cruelties of his childhood, but sensing he was still tormented by his frank and painful admission she stayed where she was, not wanting to risk upsetting him further.

Coming to a sudden standstill, he swept his still restless gaze up and down her figure. 'What made you decide to take the contraceptive in the end?' he asked.

'Why? Did you think I wouldn't take it and just pretend that I did?'

'No. I never thought you'd try and deceive me. I just…'

'What, Drake? I'm sensing there's something you want to ask me.'

'When you think about the future, do you ever think about having children?'

Breathing out a relieved sigh, Layla couldn't help smiling. 'Of course… One day I'd love to be a mum.'

'One day when the "right man" comes along, presumably?'

Now his voice was rough-edged and cynical and it made her heart bleed.

'If by the right man you mean a man that I love with all my heart and want to be with for the rest of my life, then, yes…that's when I'll be ready to become a mum.'

Drake's eyes bored into her like a laser. 'My ex-girlfriend wanted children.'

'She did?'

'That was one of the reasons we broke up. She wanted them and I didn't. And, more importantly, I didn't want to spend the rest of my life with her, so there was no way I'd make her the mother of my children. When I explained my reasons to her as diplomatically as I could, apart from accusing me of being emotionally crippled and totally insensitive for not understanding her desire for marriage and children, she said I was the most spectacularly selfish man she'd ever met and didn't doubt that I'd end up alone.'

Layla's heart bumped with sorrow and dread as she waited for him to continue.

A corner of his mouth quirked painfully. 'She was right.'

'Sometimes it helps us to have clarity when we know what we *don't* want,' she commented softly, the dread she'd felt inside that he might have stated that he would *never* want marriage or children slowly and thankfully subsiding.

'It does indeed.'

'So how *do* you feel about having children if you— if you meet the right woman?'

'It would definitely be something I'd consider.' He gave her a sheepish look. 'I used to think I'd never want a family. Maybe it's my age, but now I don't think I'd be as closed to the idea as I was before. Shall we leave it at that and get out of here for a while?'

The glimmer of some unspoken urgent idea was evident in Drake's animated gaze, and apart from what he'd just revealed about the possibility of being open to the notion of having children it made Layla's heart race.

'Why? Where do you want to go?'

'I've heard that it's going to be an exceptionally clear night. I'd like to take you to my office and show you that view of the stars through the glass roof.'

Remembering how surprised and moved she'd been when he'd told her that he sometimes turned out the lights if he was working late and the stars were bright, she felt a genuine thrill of anticipation.

'All right,' she agreed, smiling, 'I'll go and get my coat.'

'Layla?'

'Yes?'

'I didn't mean it when I accused you of being smug earlier. I was just… I was just angry that you got me to talk about that stuff. But now—now I'm glad that you did.'

Walking up to him, she gently touched his unshaven cheek with the tips of her fingers and tenderly laid her lips over his mouth. Straight away she sensed the heat they stoked into flame between them—but before she let it consume her, she lifted her head and told him, 'I think you telling me about your childhood was the bravest thing I've ever heard.'

His arms tightened possessively round her waist. 'You're good for my ego, you know that?'

Her eyes were already drifting closed, even before his lips made the fire they'd started to kindle a moment ago burst into uncontrollable flame…

CHAPTER TEN

DRAKE had laid a blanket and some cushions down on the heated wooden floor in his office, and Layla settled herself down beside him and rested her head in the crook of his arm, staring up in wonder at the cornucopia of dazzling stars that were gloriously twinkling above them through the glass ceiling. He'd been absolutely right when he'd told her that the light they emitted was so bright there was no need to turn on the lamps.

'What a genius idea to do this,' she declared enthusiastically, turning towards him.

'So it's a genius I am now, is it?'

For sheer vivacity and beauty, in Layla's opinion the sparkle in Drake's haunting grey eyes as he glanced back at her was equal to the array of stars that shone down on them. The realisation that she loved him… loved him with all her heart…struck her absolutely dumb. All she could do right then was stare into his carved handsome face and mentally imprint every beloved feature to memory, so that his image might sustain her whenever they were apart.

'What is it?' he asked, frowning, intuiting that something profound had pierced her. 'What's wrong?'

'Nothing's wrong. As a matter of fact, things couldn't be more right.'

Somehow she managed to divert him from learning the stunning realisation that had just rocked her world off its axis. She guessed that now wasn't the right time to share the news—not when he'd already had such a torrid time revisiting his agonisingly painful past. There was also a terrible fear inside her that he might not welcome her revelation—might even reject her if he wasn't ready to explore the possibility of them having a future together. *She decided that she would bide her time*.

'I'm just… I'm really enjoying myself, that's all,' she said lightly.

'Me too.' Reassured, Drake smiled and dropped an affectionate kiss onto her forehead.

For once he looked completely at ease. Even the furrows on his indomitable brow seemed more relaxed.

Layla couldn't help sighing. 'Don't you wish you could capture some of your most magical experiences and keep them for ever? I mean keep them safely locked away in a silk-lined drawer and bring them out whenever you have a bad day or simply need a pick-me-up?'

Hugging her companion's lean trim waist in the chambray shirt he wore loose over his jeans, she pressed closer into his side, breathing in his earthy masculine smell as though it was the most alluring and compelling perfume she'd ever scented.

He chuckled and she felt his fingers ruffle her hair. 'Omit the silk-lined drawer, sweetheart, and I totally concur with what you're saying. This is indeed one of those magical experiences that I'll never forget. But, for me, this whole weekend has been like that.'

'Has it? I was afraid I'd ruined everything by getting you to answer questions about your past.'

'You haven't ruined anything, and you were entitled to question me. Didn't I make a promise that I'd talk to you? I've come round to thinking that perhaps it was about time I opened up to someone about what happened when I was a kid, even though it was probably one of the hardest things I've ever done.' Drake's expression visibly softened. 'I'm glad that it was you I confided in, Layla. I wouldn't have told anyone else and that's the truth…not even a trained counsellor. My deepest darkest secrets would have gone with me to my grave.' His wry smile was reflective.

'Don't say that.' She caught his hand and urgently kissed it. 'I can't bear the thought of you being tormented by the past for the rest of your life and never telling anyone…never having any relief from the pain of it. I'm glad you agreed to talk to me, Drake, even though it was painful and difficult.' Staring deeply into his eyes, she finished, 'I'm also glad that you don't hate me for making you share your secrets with me.'

Bewildered, Drake shook his head. 'I could never hate you…no matter what you did to me. Don't you know that?'

She emitted a relieved sigh and her lips curved warmly. 'We're still friends, then?'

'Is that all you want to be to me…a friend?'

His lowered husky tone was akin to cream liqueur poured into a cup of the finest dark roast coffee…devastatingly warm and rich with a hint of luxurious velvet that was far too enticing to resist. Before Layla could reply, his lips had alighted on hers with an almost savage groan, and in the next instant his hot silken tongue was plundering the satin interior of her mouth as his big hands cupped her face and his hard-muscled body moved on top of hers, his superior weight pressing her spine deep into the luxurious woollen blanket he had lain down on the floor.

As far as Layla was concerned it might as well have been a soft feather bed. There was no sense of discomfort at all. How could there be when every ounce of her attention was intimately focused on the man who was once again taking her to a paradise she never wanted to leave, just so long as she could stay there with him for ever?

When they returned to the house and retired to bed, deliciously sated from their ardent lovemaking, Drake didn't have a single qualm about turning out the light. There was no need to wonder why he suddenly found the normally difficult task easy. The prospect of the black velvet night enveloping him and filling him with dread like it usually did didn't feature even once in his thinking…at least not with Layla lying beside him. Even though he'd fiercely resisted sharing the truth of his past with her, she had somehow broken through his iron defences to show him how sharing his story could actually *help* him banish the ghosts that haunted him— not make them even more cloying.

For the first time in years he'd discovered the true value of confiding in someone he trusted. But the most important thing that he'd learned from their heart-rending conversation was that the belief he'd had about having to deserve love was completely wrong. As a child, it had been his fundamental right to be taken care of, Layla had told him. He hadn't been denied love because he was 'bad'. It was just that his parents had been incapable of taking proper care of him, and how could that be *his* fault?

Talking about what had happened was already alleviating some of the fearful beliefs that had crippled him for too long. Consequently, with his ravishing dark-haired lover warmly enfolded in his arms, for the first time ever Drake slept the deep dreamless sleep of a man whose resentment and fear of the past was blessedly absent.

That night no dark or agonising dreams came to haunt him, and he felt like the most privileged and blessed man in the world when he woke to the joyful sound of birds singing the next morning and witnessed the sun beaming through the windows to herald a bright new day. If he didn't pride himself on being an innately logical man he might have said it was a very good omen. An omen that meant psychologically he'd turned an important corner.

Logical or not, he had the strongest urge to share his reflections with Layla. A jolt of panic knifed through him when he saw she wasn't there. Sitting bolt upright, Drake touched the sheet where her body had lain in sleep. It was still beguilingly warm. Where was she? Taking a shower?

He leapt out of bed and threw open the *en-suite* bathroom door to check. The moist shampoo-scented air in the marbled bathroom told him that she had indeed taken a shower, but had clearly moved on somewhere else. Returning to the bedroom, he pulled on a pair of clean silk boxers and dragged on his jeans. Barefoot and bare-chested, he hurried downstairs to the kitchen, calling out her name as he went.

'I'm in here,' she called back, and when Drake planted himself in the kitchen doorway she turned to him with a smile so beautiful and beguiling that he clean forgot what he'd been going to say to her.

He swallowed hard and cleared his throat, 'You're wearing my shirt again,' he observed, helplessly aroused at the sight of her long bare legs and the provocative outline of her panties, tantalisingly visible through the pristine white cotton.

'Do you mind?' Chewing down on her lip, she smoothed her still damp hair away from her face. 'I just grabbed something to put on after my shower so I could come downstairs and make us some coffee.'

'You can wear whatever you like that belongs to me.' Moving towards her, he grinned. 'Although I'd prefer it if you wore nothing at all.'

'That's not a terribly good idea when I'm boiling water.'

'Are you always so cautious?' Sliding his hands round her waist, Drake let his hungry gaze drink her in as if she was the finest wine he'd ever sampled. But even the most full-bodied Cabernet Sauvignon or French Bordeaux didn't have the power to heat his blood like Layla did.

'Sometimes not cautious enough,' she murmured, flattening her palms against his chest as if to stop him from getting any closer.

'Why? Don't you trust me?'

She lifted an amused dark eyebrow. 'Not when you

come down to the kitchen looking like you've got lascivious intentions in mind rather than wanting to enjoy a cup of my expertly made coffee.'

'Can't I have lascivious intentions *and* enjoy your expertly made coffee as well?'

'I'm sure you can. But my own intentions are to make some toast, because I'm at my hungriest in the morning. By the way, did you sleep all right last night? You certainly looked peaceful when I woke up this morning and saw you. That's why I decided to let you sleep on for a bit.'

His mouth quirked with a wry smile, 'I slept like I'd been pleasantly drugged. I can't recall having even a single dream.'

'So…there were no nightmares?'

'None.' Drake tenderly threaded his fingers through her long damp hair. 'See what a positive effect you have on me, Ms Jerome?'

'I aim to please.'

'Do you indeed?'

A self-conscious tinge of scarlet coloured her cheeks. 'Seriously, though, I'm so glad you slept better. I hope it becomes a regular feature…the start of a much more relaxed and enjoyable phase of your life. You deserve it, Drake. By the way—I've got one more question to ask you.'

'What's that?' A wave of pleasure had rolled through him at her kindness, her genuinely unselfish hopes for his future, but he had a brief moment of trepidation wondering what she might be going to ask him.

'Do you have any marmalade? It's just that it's my favourite thing to have on toast in the morning.'

His relief that her question wasn't more taxing knew no bounds. With a chuckle, he affectionately pinched the end of her nose. 'Baby I've got whatever your heart desires.'

Unable to resist impelling her against his chest, Drake felt the blood in his veins thrum hotly at the delicious sensory pleasure of her soft feminine curves next to his harder masculine body.

The big long-lashed dark eyes that he'd been so mesmerised by when he'd seen Layla for the very first time widened to saucers. 'That's a very beguiling claim, but luckily for you all I want right now is some marmalade.'

'Is that *really* all you want?' He slid his hand all the way down her slim back to rest it on her peach-shaped derrière, then pressed her against him so that she could be in no doubt about how much he wanted her. He was so aroused it was painful.

'You don't play fair,' she chastised, wagging her finger schoolmistress-like at him, her voice completely devoid of sympathy. 'As tempting as you are…as *needy* as you are…I'm afraid I'm going to have to exercise some of that bull-headedness you once accused me of because before I contemplate anything else I *really* need my breakfast.'

Before he could stop her she'd wriggled out of his arms and headed for the bread-bin atop the kitchen counter. He knew it contained the brown seeded loaf that he'd bought at the deli along with their croissants yesterday. Sighing, he realised he would manfully have to subdue his desire—at least until she'd had her breakfast. Clearly there was no stopping the woman when her

mind was set on something. His feelings were a pro-
voking mix of frustration and affection.

'I'd be a poor host indeed if I didn't let you eat.' He
smiled and, moving across to the large American-style
fridge, extracted an unopened pot of marmalade. 'Why
don't you make the coffee and let me do the toast?' he
suggested. 'After that we'll—'

'Go back to bed?' Layla's chocolate-brown eyes met
his with an unwavering amused stare that made Drake's
heart miss a beat.

'My thoughts exactly,' he agreed huskily.

It was hard for Layla to accept that their time together
was coming to an end. Having already explained that
he probably wouldn't be able to see her this week, due
to his colossal workload—not least of all their town's
pressing and much needed regeneration—Drake had
definitely looked unhappy when he'd told her. Telling
herself she'd just have to accept his absence and pray
that the following week might yield a greater possibility of them seeing each other again, Layla fell silent as
he drove them home, not trusting herself in case she
broke down and confessed that she loved him.

*Why did the prospect of saying goodbye to him this
evening feel like a death sentence?* she wondered miserably. They'd had such a wonderful day together—
laughing and talking and making love till they were
breathless and sated, then somehow finding the energy
to go down to the kitchen and make themselves something to eat. It didn't seem right that they should be
parted for even an hour, let alone a whole week!

'Before I drop you home I'd like to show you something.' Drake's handsome carved profile was disconcertingly serious as he stared out through the windscreen, making the necessary turn that would take them out of the near deserted high street.

The only occupants in evidence were a couple of local teenagers leaning against a galvanised steel grille shop-front, smoking. Compared to the wealthy and elite part of the capital she and Drake had just come from, the shabby provincial town seemed even more rundown and drab than it usually did.

'Show me what?' Layla asked, unable to suppress the feeling of inexplicable apprehension that coiled in the pit of her stomach.

'The house where I grew up.'

He spared her a brief unreadable glance just as she registered that they were approaching the small shabby side-street whose abandoned terraced houses he planned to tear down and replace with modern ones. The house he drew up outside was a dismal grey terrace with all the windows shattered and broken and a large 'Keep Out' sign emblazoned across the dingy charcoal-grey front door. The stone steps that led to the once fashionable arched brick entrance were covered in litter and broken beer bottles, she saw. No doubt some of the population of jobless teenagers and youths hung out there, she thought.

Unsure about what to say, she laid her hand across Drake's, not moving it even when she sensed him flinch uncomfortably.

Now that she knew something of his unhappy past, she hoped visiting the street wouldn't bombard him with tormenting memories. It wasn't hard to imagine what he must be thinking, and no doubt that was why he was so determined to demolish the houses rather than have them renovated. Did he hope that when the houses were smashed to smithereens it would likewise crush the hurtful nightmares of his past? Last night she'd been so encouraged when he'd been able to turn out the light and sleep more easily, and she didn't doubt that trend would continue if only he could realise he wasn't to blame for what had happened to him as a child…that he'd always deserved to be loved just as much as anyone else did.

'It's funny,' he murmured, 'but it looks so much smaller and insignificant than it did when I was a child. If my dad was still alive I bet he'd look smaller and insignificant too.'

'If the thought helps you no longer see him as an ogre, and you can start to put your disturbing memories of him to bed, then I'm glad you think that. But I'm sure that if he could see you now and learn what a successful and wealthy man you've become—through all your own efforts too—he would be proud…even if he couldn't bring himself to show it.'

A muscle flinched in the side of Drake's lean, carved cheekbone, conveying the undoubted tension in his body. 'The old bastard was too mean to be proud of anyone or anything…especially his son. He was totally self-obsessed. But thanks for the thought just the same.'

Grimacing, Layla didn't shy away from the bitterness and sorrow she heard in his tone and lapse into silence. Instead an even stronger determination to stay as positive as possible and not collude with his misery arose inside her. 'You know if it was renovated along with all the others in the street this house could potentially be very nice. Was it in such a sorry state as it is now when you lived here with your dad?' she asked.

Sighing heavily, Drake shook his head. 'It was always rundown, but not as bad as it is now, thank God. As I got older I used to try and keep it free from litter at least. And the windows never got broken because it was my job to clean them. I didn't dare risk kicking a football around outside and potentially ruining all my hard work. Even then I longed for my surroundings to be beautiful.'

Helplessly picturing the small boy who'd taken on the household jobs his father should have assumed, in a bid to maintain some sort of pleasing exterior to what must have been his desperately unhappy interior life, Layla grimaced again. 'Has it helped you coming back here to see it again?' she asked softly.

'Who knows?' The expression in his haunting grey eyes was far away for a moment. 'Only time will tell. The point is I didn't want to hide anything from you—that's why I brought you here. I wanted you to see for yourself the house and the environment I grew up in. I wanted to be truthful and show you exactly where I came from…who I really am.'

'I feel privileged that you trust me enough to show me, Drake. But who you really are isn't defined by your past, you know. You can write a new script every day… every moment, in fact. It didn't happen overnight, but recently I've come to realise that myself. Thinking about how my boss ripped me off just keeps me stuck in the same miserable, unhappy story. It doesn't help me move on and enjoy my life, and just because we've been hurt by someone in the past it doesn't mean that everyone we meet in the future is going to hurt us.'

'I'm sure you're right.' Drake's steady glance was deeply thoughtful for a moment. 'I've got something I want to tell you before I take you home.'

'What's that?'

'I'm not going to have the houses demolished after all. I'm going to have them renovated, as you suggested.'

Layla was speechless. Then, as hope and elation poured through her at the same time, she smiled at Drake and said, 'You *are*? What changed your mind?'

'You did, Layla. You made me see things differently. I've begun to wonder if this regeneration of the town isn't a good opportunity for me to bury the ghosts of the past and start over. I have the means and the know how to help others who live here have a better and more beautiful environment that might inspire them to do something good with their lives instead of feeling hopeless, and that's exactly what I plan to do. I'm also going to turn my old house into that youth club you suggested the town needs.'

'You mean it?'

'Absolutely.'

'I can hardly believe it,' Sighing, Layla slowly shook her head in wonder. 'I'm so proud of you, Drake…so proud. I don't doubt that given time you're going to make a huge difference to people's lives with all you plan to do here.'

'Talking of time—I ought to get you home.'

Lifting her hand in a gentlemanly gesture that might have come straight out of a Regency novel, he brushed his lips against her fingers with almost polite restraint.

Even then Layla realised the heat between them was but a mere breath away, and could be ignited by one unguarded glance, let alone a touch. Breathing out slowly, she somehow found a smile—no easy task when she knew they would soon have to say goodbye to each other. She honestly wondered how she would survive the next few days without seeing him.

As if the same realisation had suddenly occurred to him, Drake clenched his jaw and gunned the engine. But as the car sped along the dark shabby streets Layla believed that he would indeed put the ghosts of his troubled past behind him and truly start afresh. He'd told her she had helped him see things differently. *Did that include her assertion that he could write a new script for his life?* Whether the idea would help him reflect on the possibility of a brighter future with her, she could only hope and pray…

'It's the house on the right-hand side.'

'You mean the large Victorian?'

'That's right.'

Driving through the well-kept streets on the much more affluent side of town, Drake felt the pit of his stomach churn helplessly. From her description of where she lived, he'd already guessed that Layla's upbringing had been a million miles away from his own. Without even hearing her address he only had to remember the kindness of her father who'd run the newsagents to know that she'd been well taken care of. There was also the brother who adored her…the brother who was determined to make a currently unprofitable coffee house a roaring success, and had given her a job when her sleazebag employer had swindled her out of her savings. Who wouldn't be envious of having a sibling like that to rely on?

After spending such an unbelievably joyous weekend with Layla, he hated the insecurity that suddenly seized him. The prospect of not seeing her again for an entire week didn't help. Following her out of the car, Drake struggled hard to win back his equilibrium.

'Will you come in and have a coffee with me before you head back to London?' she asked him, her tone hinting at her uncertainty that he might not.

'That would be great.' Determinedly finding a reassuring smile, he reached for her hand. *Didn't she know that the prospect of spending a little more time with her made him feel as wildly happy as a prisoner on death row who'd been given an unbelievable last minute reprieve?*

As they climbed the steps to the impressive porch of the house the scarlet front door opened from the inside and Marc, Layla's tousle-headed brother, appeared to greet them.

'The wanderer returns.' He immediately stepped forward to envelop his sister in a hard warm hug, and Drake had no choice but to let go of her hand. The cold stab of jealousy that slashed through his insides at being forced to relinquish her even for a moment almost made him feel physically sick it was so strong.

'Are you okay?' The other man wore a frown as he held Layla at arm's length to examine her. 'I tried God only knows how many times over the weekend to reach you, but you'd obviously turned off your phone.' He glanced warily at Drake over her shoulder. 'I tried your mobile as well, but that was turned off too. Anyone would think the two of you had disappeared off the planet!'

Drake's gaze tumbled helplessly into Layla's and their eyes exchanged a very private signal of mutual understanding. 'We stayed on the planet, but I don't deny we shut out the world for a couple of days,' he drawled, low-voiced.

'I was perfectly fine, Marc,' Layla cut in quickly. 'You know I'm quite capable of taking care of myself, so there was absolutely no need for you to worry. Now, I'm going upstairs to my flat to make Drake and me a cup of coffee. Do you want to join us?'

'Thanks all the same, but I won't. The accounts beckon, I'm afraid. By the way—I made a couple of Victoria sponges to take into the café tomorrow. Help yourself if you'd like some with your coffee. It's nice to see you again, Drake...even if you did kidnap my beautiful sister for the weekend!'

'It's good to see you too,' Drake murmured, right then feeling anything *but* friendly towards the other man.

He was glad to be invited upstairs to Layla's flat so that they could have some privacy. Back at the house in Mayfair, he'd asked her if she thought his home lacked warmth. Glancing round the cosy living-room in her flat, with its sandalwood-scented air, homely feminine touches, mismatched furniture, family portraits on the walls and enough candles in the fireplace to light a cathedral, it wasn't a question she would ever have to ask him. Her home was an irresistibly warm expression of the lovely woman who inhabited it, and Drake was suddenly unsure about the hopes he'd subconsciously been nurturing over the weekend.

What could he possibly offer a woman like Layla, apart from what his material wealth could provide? he wondered. Having come into contact with her generous heart and concern for others, he doubted whether that would even be an inducement. Why would she want to leave a home she loved with a brother who adored and looked out for her to move up to London and live with him? he mused. Especially when her experience of living and working there previously had been indelibly soured by an unscrupulous boss who had swindled her out of her life savings and seduced her. Wasn't that why she had retreated from city life in the first place? To lick her wounds in a place of safety?

As sure as night followed day, and despite his plans to regenerate the town and improve it, Drake certainly wouldn't contemplate returning to live with her, no matter how strong his feelings were. And even if they could agree on a mutually acceptable place of residence if they got together permanently, what if one day Layla walked out on him, just as his mother had? What if she made that soul-destroying decision because she'd reached the same conclusion his ex had made about him...that he was 'emotionally crippled' and—despite his wealth and success—a poor bet if he couldn't shake his past? *Could he risk such a devastating possibility and be left to live his life without her?*

'Do you fancy a slice of Victoria sponge with your coffee?' As she returned to the living room from the kitchen Layla's cheerful voice broke into his bleak introspection.

'No, thanks.' He gave an awkward shrug of the shoulders. 'In fact, I don't think I'll stay and have coffee after all. I've had my mobile switched off since Friday night, and I've probably got at least fifty or sixty messages I need to reply to.'

Her lovely face was immediately crestfallen, and Drake felt like the very worst criminal.

'Can't you stay for just half an hour longer? Surely that won't make a lot of difference? In any case, it won't be late by the time you get back to London. You'll have plenty of time to answer your messages then,' she pointed out reasonably.

Her suggestion was more than tempting, but he had already made up his mind to go. They had spent an amazing and intense time together, but now he needed some space and time alone to get his head straight.

Without thinking he moved across the room and took her into his arms. 'I'm sorry, sweetheart, I really am. But I've got a heavy week ahead of me and there are plans and drawings I need to study, as well as replying to my phone messages. We'll see each other again very soon…I promise. I'll ring you just as soon as I know when I can take some time off.'

Her dark eyes looked alternately sad, then resigned. That disappointed and melancholy glance made Drake feel as though someone had punched him hard in the gut.

'If for some reason you can't reach me on my mobile you can leave a message with Marc, either here or at the café,' she told him, her tongue moistening her lips as if they'd suddenly turned dry.

'Great.' His fingers firmed possessively round her

slim upper arms, the warmth of her satin skin provocatively evident in the sheer silk blouse he had bought her. Desolation settled in the pit of his stomach at the thought of sleeping in his bed tonight without her. 'It's been an incredible weekend and I've loved every minute of it being with you, Layla,' he told her honestly, his voice low.

In answer, her pretty lips curved to form the sweetest smile. 'I'll never forget lying on the blanket in your office looking up at the stars through that amazing glass ceiling,' she admitted softly.

'We'll do it again some time soon. That's a promise.'

'I'll hold you to that.' Reaching up on tiptoe, she pressed her lips gently against his. 'You'd better go before I make a complete fool of myself and cry,' she said.

Forcing himself to ignore the instinct to plunder and ravish her mouth, as he longed to do, Drake slowly nodded his head. 'Thanks for everything,' he murmured, reluctantly extricating himself from their embrace and walking to the door.

'It was my pleasure,' Layla murmured, and he turned briefly to give her a smile...

CHAPTER ELEVEN

LAYLA threw herself into a frenzy of activity in a bid to try and keep her anxious thoughts about Drake at bay. When she wasn't working at the café, serving the trickle of customers that came in throughout the day and keeping it spick and span, she was tidying and de-cluttering her flat, and driving the laden boxes of clothes and bric-a-brac she'd collected to a charity shop in support of sick children. After that, she avidly perused her cookery books to come up with new and enticing recipes that she could cook for herself and Marc.

It was only in the unguarded moments that sneaked up on her from time to time that the memory of Drake—how he looked, the sound of his voice, how it felt when he took her in his arms—had the ability to make her catch her breath and her body ache with longing.

As the interminably long week progressed she relived time and time again the frighteningly naked and poignant smile he'd left her with, wishing she'd had the courage to ask him there and then what was really on his mind. Was it that he'd decided he didn't want to commit to a relationship with her after all now that he'd revealed so much about his wounded past? Because it made him feel far too exposed and vulnerable? Didn't he know that she'd rather *die* than betray him by sharing what he'd told her with anyone else?

When the working week drew to a close without any word from him at all, Layla determinedly resisted the overwhelming urge to ring *him*. Instead she drove to the building site where Drake had taken her that day to explain his plans for the area's improvement, in the no doubt unrealistic hope that he might be there. *He wasn't.*

When she arrived she saw straight away that the construction workers had clearly shut up shop for the day. The muddied landscape and recently erected scaffolding looked bleak, cold and abandoned…*the description could well have been applied to her.*

Back in her flat, she nearly jumped out of her skin when the hallway telephone rang. Abandoning the removal of her jacket, she haphazardly shrugged it back onto her shoulders and urgently grabbed the receiver.

It was him…it *had* to be him.

'Hello?'

'Layla? It's me—Colette.'

She'd never been so disappointed to hear the voice of a friend. It was a loyal pal she occasionally enjoyed 'girly' nights in with—drinking wine, putting the world to rights and giggling over the latest rom-com together.

'Hi,' she answered, her hand shaking from the onrush of adrenaline that had poured through her when she'd thought the caller might be Drake. 'How nice to hear from you. It's been a while. How are you?'

'I'm good. How about you?'

'I'm fine, thanks.' It grieved Layla that she wasn't able to sound more convincing. A girl needed her friends—especially at times like these—and Colette was a good one.

'Hmm…' the other girl commented. 'You don't sound fine to me. Want to talk about what's been going on?'

Was she a mind-reader? Flushing guiltily, Layla absently curled some silky dark strands of hair round her ear. 'I've met someone, that's all.'

There was a pause, then Colette asked wondrously, 'You mean you've met a man you're crazy about?'

'How did you know?'

'Because if you weren't crazy about him you wouldn't even tell me you'd met someone. You're not a girl who indulges in casual meaningless encounters… or casual meaningless sex, for that matter. I've always sensed that when you finally met a guy you were genuinely attracted to it would have to be all or nothing. Who is he and where did you meet him?'

Feeling protective of Drake's privacy, and how much or how little she could safely reveal about him, Layla examined the short unvarnished fingernails she'd recently taken to nibbling and sighed. 'I met him here… in the town.'

'Is he local?'

'No. He lives and works in London.'

'What on earth was he doing here, then?'

The incredulity in her friend's voice didn't surprise her. Their town was hardly the jewel of the county…at least not *yet*. 'Working… He's part of the professional team that's working on the regeneration.'

'So he's a town planner or surveyor, perhaps?'

She swallowed hard. 'Something like that.'

'Okaay… I can tell you're being more than a little protective of him… Got any plans for tonight?'

'No…I don't.' Layla wished she was planning on getting ready to see Drake, and it hurt more than she could say that she wasn't.

'That's settled, then. I can tell you're in need of some friendly advice and support. As soon as I get ready, and pop into the off-licence on the way for a cracking bottle of wine, I'll be round to pay you a visit. And don't worry about searching through your collection for a film…we'll have far too much to chat about for that! Bye for now. I'll see you soon.'

As she heard the line disconnect at the other end Layla stared blankly at the wall, wondering miserably if she could summon up the energy to share confidences with a well-meaning friend when in all honesty she'd much rather crawl under the duvet and cry…

He'd sat in the car outside the house for almost ten minutes, mentally rehearsing what he was going to say to her. The first hurdle Drake had to cross was whether Layla was actually in, because he hadn't phoned ahead to let her know he was coming. When he'd seen the lights shining from the windows of the upper floor he had murmured a fervent and relieved, 'Thank God…' and told himself that fate must be on his side after all.

Now that he was here he could hardly believe he'd so foolishly stayed away from her for an entire week. Yes, he had genuinely had a workload that barely gave him time to draw breath, but the real reason he hadn't rung her was because he'd had a nagging story running in his head about her being unwilling to compromise on what she wanted. Consequently he'd allowed the twin gremlins of doubt and fear to prevent him from taking the courageous step he needed to.

This morning, for the first time in days, Drake had woken with the clarity of mind he'd prayed for and his heart filled with absolute certainty about what he should do. But now that he was here, sitting outside the gracious Victorian house that Layla had grown up in, he suddenly felt unsure again. *After all, there was no guarantee that she'd be happy to see him, was there?* Not after he'd so abruptly cut their last evening together short without any real explanation. What if she thought he was a terrible coward…even *worse* an unreliable bastard?

'Damn!' A colourful expletive followed his frustrated exclamation, and hurriedly stepping out onto the pavement from the Aston Martin that he'd told Jimmy he would drive himself that evening, he closed the door shut with a slam.

Straightening the blue silk tie he wore with his tailored suit, he climbed the wide stone steps up to the front door, his heart hammering harder than if he'd received a prestigious commission from the Queen herself. When he rang the bell, and shortly afterwards saw the hallway light come on through the frosted panes in the door, he stood there in dry-mouthed anticipation of seeing Layla again, fervently hoping that nothing would jinx the event.

'Well, well, well—as you said to me when I paid a surprise visit to your office… To what do I owe the honour?'

Dressed in black skinny jeans and a biscuit-coloured

cardigan, with her feet bare, Layla flashed her glossy brown eyes as if Drake was the last person on earth she'd expected or indeed wanted to see. But her less-than-warm welcome made him even more determined to get her to see reason, and his avid gaze roamed her beautiful features with a slow, teasing smile.

'If I tell you that this past week I've missed you more than I've ever missed anyone or anything in my life will that get me an invite in for the cup of coffee I so foolishly declined when I was last here?' he asked, his voice pitched intimately low.

She was still holding onto the doorframe, as if undecided whether to let him over the threshold or not, but there was a glimmer of what he took to be hope in her eyes, and the majority of the tension that had been making his insides ache for days slowly ebbed.

'That's all you want? A cup of coffee?' she quizzed warily.

'A cup of your expertly made coffee would be a start, I suppose.'

'A start to what, exactly?'

'I'm hoping a frank and truthful conversation.'

'That's what I'd like too. Okay. But I'm afraid you're going to have to wait until my friend leaves. She's popped round to give me a little female support.'

Drake frowned. 'Support for what?'

Her cheeks turned engagingly pink. 'There are times when we women need a good friend to turn to. This is one of those times.'

'Are you saying that you needed to discuss you and me?' he asked warily.

'What do you think? Did it even cross your mind that

I might be feeling a little low after you left so abruptly on Sunday? We were getting on so well—you even took me back to the street where you grew up and told me about your plan to renovate the houses instead of pulling them down. But then…then we came back here and you suddenly decided you had to leave. I haven't discussed anything personal with Colette, but I was planning on telling her that I'd met someone that I— Anyway.' She flushed and glanced down at the floor for a second. 'That's when the doorbell rang. You couldn't have timed your arrival more perfectly if you'd tried.'

'And what were you going to tell your friend, I wonder? That I took you back to my house, mercilessly seduced you, then took you home and hurriedly made my exit, never to be seen or heard of again?'

Drake tried and failed to keep the angry hurt from his tone. More than he hated the idea of having Layla discuss him with her friend, he abhorred the idea that she might believe he could indeed be so callous.

Her face fell. 'I would *never* have described what happened between us like that. Did you honestly think that I would?'

'Look…can I come in? Can't you tell Colleen, or whatever her name is, that I've driven down from London especially to see you and I really need us to talk?'

The mere idea of Layla having to entertain her friend when he was near desperate to clear the air between them and tell her his feelings made Drake feel tense and impatient again.

In an aggrieved tone she answered, 'If you're in that much of a hurry to talk to me, why couldn't you have rung me earlier in the week to let me know you were coming this evening? And, by the way, it's Colette—*not* Colleen. She's a good friend, and I don't get to see her that often. I won't risk offending her by asking her to leave just because *you've* suddenly decided you need to talk to me!'

'Okay.' Forcing down his deep disappointment, Drake lifted and dropped his shoulders resignedly. 'I'll just wait until she goes, then…if that's all right with you, I mean?'

'You'd better come in.'

Removing her hand from the doorframe, Layla stood back to allow him entry into the hall. As she went past him to shut the door he had to curl his hand into a fist to stop himself reaching out to touch the shining curtain of dark hair that fell onto her shoulders. *Was it only a few short days ago that he'd had the incredible good fortune to do such a thing with impunity?*

'Let's go upstairs. Colette was about to open the bottle of wine she brought with her. Perhaps you'd like a glass?'

'I think I'll decline. I want to keep a clear head this evening.'

'I'll just make you some coffee, then.'

'That would be great…thanks.'

When his avid gaze fell into hers for a full uninterrupted second, the cascade of heat and hunger that assailed him almost made Drake stumble, and his heart thumped hard when he saw by her darkening pupils that Layla was fighting a similar battle.

'I should have rung you,' he confessed huskily, 'but

I wanted to get my head straight. I had a lot to think over. Can you forgive me?'

'You're here now, and that's all that matters.'

Her gentle smile was like a wisp of ephemeral smoke—there one minute and gone the next. But, having seen it, he couldn't help but feel reassured.

At the top of the stairs a pretty young woman with gently waving blonde hair, wearing a tan-coloured raincoat over a smart blouse and jeans, stood waiting for them.

'You're not leaving, Colette?' Layla asked, startled.

'Sweetheart, you don't need me to hang around now. I didn't mean to eavesdrop, but I guessed when I heard a man's voice that it must be the guy you were going to tell me about.' She glanced up at Drake with a smile, 'I'm Layla's friend Colette.' She reached out and shook his hand, adding, 'And you are…?'

'Drake.' He didn't hesitate to give his real name, because something in the girl's frank blue eyes told him that she was fiercely loyal to Layla. 'Drake Ashton.'

'You're the famous architect that's helping to regenerate the town?'

He grimaced. 'I'm just one of a group of professionals that's been commissioned.'

The blonde's eyes twinkled mischievously. 'And are any of the other professionals as fit as you, Drake?'

'Colette!' Layla shook her head in disbelief at her friend's daring.

'Don't worry, Drake, I'm only teasing. Layla knows I'm very happily married, and right now I'm going to head back home and suggest that my other half and I go out for a nice romantic meal somewhere. Why don't the two of you open that bottle of wine I brought and enjoy it on me?'

Noticing that Layla was frowning, as though concerned that her friend felt under pressure to cut short her visit, Drake caught her hand and gave it a reassuring squeeze. 'I promise that the next time you and Colette arrange a girls' night in I won't break up your evening by demanding you spend time with me instead.'

'That's settled, then. I'm going.' The blonde gave him a satisfied conspiratorial wink.

'And the bottle of wine is on me next time, Colette,' he promised.

'I'll hold you to that. Just make sure the two of you have some fun tonight, won't you? And there's just one more thing, Drake…'

'What's that?'

'Don't break her heart. Trust me, you're a very lucky man that she's interested in you. I was beginning to wonder if she'd ever find someone she really liked.'

His eyes lit on Layla in a penetrating gaze. 'Rest assured I don't take her for granted.'

Tearing her glance from his, Layla stepped round him to give her friend an affectionate hug. 'Thanks for coming over. I'll give you a ring very soon, I promise.'

'I'll look forward to it. Bye, sweetie.'

As soon as she and Drake were alone again, Layla walked in silence back into the flat. It disturbed him that she appeared so ill at ease. *Did she really have no idea how he felt?* Following her into the kitchen, he glanced at the unopened bottle of wine standing on the counter. Standing beside it were two slim-stemmed glasses and a corkscrew.

'I know I said I'd have coffee, but shall we break the ice by having a glass of wine?' he suggested lightly, hunting for a way to help her relax.

'Break the ice?' Layla rounded on him with a disbelieving glare. 'Has our relationship become so brittle since we last saw each other that we need an icebreaker to help us communicate? I for one would rather just get straight to the point.'

'I agree. Why don't we do just that?'

'You agree?'

Resisting the urge to smile, because she looked so damn adorable right then, Drake threw up his hands in a gesture of surrender. 'I do. Why don't you go first and tell me what you've been thinking?'

'All right, then. I will.' Folding her arms, she moved restlessly across the black and white tiled floor and back again. 'Something happened when you dropped me back home on Sunday. You were going to stay for coffee, but then you suddenly changed your mind. Personally, I don't believe your urgent departure had anything to do with work or having to return your phone messages. Something about being in my home made you uncomfortable. What was it, Drake? Did you suddenly fear I'd make some sort of demand on you that you didn't want or perhaps didn't feel ready to meet? Or maybe it was that you wished you hadn't shown me where you'd grown up because it made you feel too vulnerable?'

Wincing, Drake pushed his fingers through his hair and nodded slowly. 'I didn't fear you making demands on me, Layla. But you're right… I *did* have reservations about showing you my old home…at least the first time. The second time we went back I was less tense, because I wanted to tell you that I'd changed my mind about tearing the houses down...that I had decided to renovate instead. But when we came back here and I saw that you'd grown up in a much better part of town than I had...and in such a beautiful home...the home you share with a brother who clearly means the world to you and who clearly adores you too... I wondered what I could possibly offer you that would be an incentive for you to exchange all that simply to be with me?'

Sweeping her fringe back off her face, Layla knew her expression was genuinely stunned. 'You seriously don't *know* what you could offer me that would be an incentive to stay with you?'

His heartbeat accelerated, making it hard for him to articulate his feelings. He drew in a deep breath to steady himself. 'Let's look at the facts, shall we? You have a lovely home here—a home full of warm family memories that you understandably returned to when things turned sour for you in London. You'd probably never consider living in the city again, and even though I came back here to help with the town's regeneration and improve it I'm sure you can understand why it's not a place I would personally ever want to live in again.'

'Going back to what you were saying before. Are you telling me that you *want* me to stay with you, Drake? I mean...as in *living* with you?'

His mouth drying, he moved across the room to stand in front of her. 'Yes...that's exactly what I'm saying, Layla.'

Her soft cheeks flushed rosily. 'Why? *Why* do you want me to live with you?'

The blood in Drake's veins thundered hotly in embarrassment when he realised she didn't know. Instead of telling her how he felt, as he'd planned to do, he'd somehow lulled himself into believing she would intuit everything. Grimacing, he silently made a vow that he would never let fear and doubt stop him from confessing his true feelings to this woman ever again.

He touched his palm to her cheek and held it there, loving the sensation of her warm satin skin. 'I want you to live with me because I'm crazy about you…crazy to the point of feeling like you've put me under some kind of spell. Even when I'm supposed to be working I can't stop thinking about you. What I'm trying to tell you is that I love you, Layla. I love you more than I ever dreamed it was possible to love anyone, and I don't want to blow my one chance at real happiness by letting you go. If you can't live in London, and I can't live here, then we're just going to have to come up with some mutually agreeable compromise.'

Her beautiful dark eyes danced teasingly. 'What makes you think I'd never consider living in London with you?'

Frowning, Drake rested his hands either side of her svelte hips and couldn't resist the compelling urge to bring her closer into his body. 'That low-life of a boss of yours must have hurt you badly with what he did. I perfectly understand why the memory of such a painful experience might put you off the idea of living there. I also understand why it means a lot to you to live *here*. For one thing, apart from the happy memories of your childhood, your brother's here. Not only that, you've got a job working for him. I doubt that you'd agree to resign to come and live with me, would you?'

'You seem to think you know a lot about what I want and don't want, don't you? Will you give me the chance to tell you what I want myself?'

'Of course.'

Emitting a soft breath, Layla smiled. 'First of all, I love you too, Drake… I didn't know it at the time, but maybe it happened when your incredible grey eyes looked back into mine that very first time? I never dreamt I'd fall for someone so hard and so fast, and at first it scared me. It scared me a lot. But the truth is I'd live anywhere you wanted me to just so long as I could be with you. And as for Marc—I'm sure I can persuade him to rent out my flat to help him make some extra money to pay off his debts, and also to give the café some much needed redecoration.'

'What about your job there?'

'I was thinking I'd keep it until the town project comes to an end. I don't mean I'll stay living here, if you want me to move in with you sooner, but when the regeneration is complete I'll get a job somewhere local to wherever we're living.' Pausing, she reached up to gently push some hair back from his forehead. 'There's one more thing I want to tell you. When I lost my life savings I didn't really lose anything of value…at least not in the sense of *true* value. Even though I was upset and demoralised by it at the time, after I moved back here I started to realise I should be grateful for what I *had*…not mourn what I'd lost. And for me it's always been the people I love that I value the most.'

Capturing her hand, Drake brought it up to his lips

and planted a warm lingering kiss in the centre of her palm. 'You are one incredible woman—you know that?'

'No, I'm not. It's you who's incredible. To come back here and help bring hope and new life to the community by improving the town after your sad experiences growing up here…well, it's *beyond* brave in my book. Why *did* you decide to take the commission, by the way? You've never told me.'

He thought hard for a moment, wanting to be absolutely truthful. 'I suppose subconsciously I was looking to reinvent my relationship with the place…to bury my regrets and turn my memories into much more positive ones. When I was first contacted about working on the regeneration my instinct was not to touch it with a bargepole. But I forced myself to think more deeply about it, and in the end I decided to take it on for the very reasons I just explained. Seeing as that decision brought me to you, Layla, I'm guaranteed the good memories I always secretly craved. I never thought for one moment that I'd find the most beautiful girl in the world living here, and that I'd instantly fall in love with her, but I did…I *did*. It really is a dream come true.'

'I'm just ordinary, Drake…hardly the most beautiful girl in the world.'

'Sweetheart, you're going to have to learn to take compliments if you're going to be with me, because I plan to shower you with them every day throughout our long and happy marriage.' He smiled.

This astounding announcement put Layla's mind into a dizzying spin and made her heart clamour wildly. 'You want to *marry* me?' she asked incredulously.

'Just as soon as it can be arranged—and I won't be

slow to pull a few favours from the official powers-that-be to help me achieve that, I promise you.'

'There's one more thing I'd like to ask you.'

'What's that?'

This time when he responded to the notion of her asking what might be another personal question he didn't look remotely wary or defensive, Layla noticed. Instead his glance was infinitely warm and understanding.

'Not jumping the gun or anything…but would you really consider us having children?'

'Would you believe me if I told you that when I realised I might have made you pregnant I honestly considered asking you to go ahead and have the child if there was one? When you told me you'd taken that emergency contraceptive I felt like I'd been robbed of an incredible opportunity that I'd never even realised was important to me.'

Feeling her heart melt, Layla couldn't disguise the wondrous happiness she felt at his words. 'I'd love to have your baby—you know that? Because I know you'll be the most incredibly loving and inspirational father. In which case I'm guessing I should definitely say yes to your proposal, shouldn't I?'

She didn't have a chance to say anything else right then, because Drake lowered his head to hers and kissed her with a hunger that wouldn't be sated until they both capitulated to the desperate need to be even closer—a desperately wild and passionate need that would always be a feature of their marriage until they were old, Layla guessed happily…

* * * * *

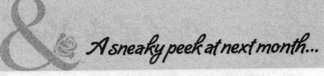

A sneaky peek at next month...

MODERN™

INTERNATIONAL AFFAIRS, SEDUCTION & PASSION GUARANTEED

My wish list for next month's titles...

In stores from 21st December 2012:

❏ Beholden to the Throne — Carol Marinelli

❏ Her Little White Lie — Maisey Yates

❏ The Incorrigible Playboy — Emma Darcy

❏ The Enigmatic Greek — Catherine George

In stores from 4th January 2013:

❏ The Petrelli Heir — Kim Lawrence

❏ Her Shameful Secret — Susanna Carr

❏ No Longer Forbidden? — Dani Collins

❏ The Night That Started It All — Anna Cleary

❏ The Secret Wedding Dress — Ally Blake

Available at WHSmith, Tesco, Asda, Eason, Amazon and Apple

Just can't wait?

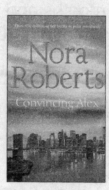

The World of Mills & Boon®

There's a Mills & Boon® series that's perfect for you. We publish ten series and, with new titles every month, you never have to wait long for your favourite to come along.

Blaze.
Scorching hot, sexy reads
4 new stories every month

By Request
Relive the romance with the best of the best
9 new stories every month

Cherish™
Romance to melt the heart every time
12 new stories every month

Desire™
Passionate and dramatic love stories
8 new stories every month

Visit us Online
Try something new with our Book Club offer
www.millsandboon.co.uk/freebookoffer

What will you treat yourself to next?

Ignite your imagination,
step into the past…
6 new stories every month

INTRIGUE…

Breathtaking romantic suspense
Up to 8 new stories every month

Medical Romance

Captivating medical drama –
with heart
6 new stories every month

MODERN™

International affairs,
seduction & passion guaranteed
9 new stories every month

n o c t u r n e™

Deliciously wicked
paranormal romance
Up to 4 new stories every month

RIVA™

Live life to the full –
give in to temptation
3 new stories every month available
exclusively via our Book Club

Have Your Say

*You've just finished your book.
So what did you think?*

We'd love to hear your thoughts on our
'Have your say' online panel
www.millsandboon.co.uk/haveyoursay

- 🌹 Easy to use
- 🌹 Short questionnaire
- 🌹 Chance to win Mills & Boon® goodies

Visit us Online | Tell us what you thought of this book now at
www.millsandboon.co.uk/haveyoursay

YOUR_SAY